Frayed Edges

a quilting cozy

Carol Dean Jones

Publisher: Amy Barrett-Daffin

Creative Director / Technical Editor: Gailen Runge

Acquisitions Editor: Roxane Cerda

Managing Editor: Liz Aneloski

Project Writer: Teresa Stroin

Cover/Book Designer: April Mostek

Production Coordinator: Zinnia Heinzmann

Production Editor: Alice Mace Nakanishi

Illustrator: Aliza Shalit

Photo Assistant: Lauren Herberg

Cover photography by Estefany Gonzalez of C&T Publishing, Inc.

Cover quilt: *Frayed Edges*, 2020, by the author

Published by C&T Publishing, Inc.,
P.O. Box 1456, Lafayette, CA 94549

Library of Congress Cataloging-in-Publication Data

Names: Jones, Carol Dean, author.

Title: Frayed edges : a quilting cozy / Carol Dean Jones.

Description: Lafayette, CA : C&T Publishing, [2021] | Series: A quilting cozy ; 12

Identifiers: LCCN 2020053409 | ISBN 9781644031056 (trade paperback) | ISBN 9781644031063 (ebook)

Subjects: GSAFD: Mystery fiction.

Classification: LCC PS3610.O6224 F73 2021 | DDC 813/.6--dc23

LC record available at https://lccn.loc.gov/2020053409

POD Edition

A Quilting Cozy Series

by Carol Dean Jones

Tie Died (book 1)

Running Stitches (book 2)

Sea Bound (book 3)

Patchwork Connections (book 4)

Stitched Together (book 5)

Moon Over the Mountain (book 6)

The Rescue Quilt (book 7)

Missing Memories (book 8)

Tattered & Torn (book 9)

Left Holding the Bag (book 10)

Beneath Missouri Stars (book 11)

Frayed Edges (book 12)

Dedication

To Sharon and Butch Rose,
whose friendship I cherish

Acknowledgments

I want to thank four special friends: Sharon Rose, Jan Packard, Paula Curran, and Joyce Frazier. These talented women spent endless hours reading and rereading this manuscript, locating my omissions and inconsistencies, and making valuable recommendations.

I also want to thank the staff of C&T Publishing for their support and commitment to publishing and marketing my Quilting Cozy series. Special thanks go to Roxane Cerda, who is always there for me.

But the bulk of my appreciation goes to my many loyal readers who have stuck by me through all twelve books in this series, consistently asking for more. You've bonded with my characters, as have I, and I appreciate your many emails and blog comments.

Chapter 1

When I think of the time and love poured into making these quilts long ago, and the many loved ones who were kept warm and cozy beneath them, I understand that their beauty is not only in the hand stitching and the old fabrics; it is also in the frayed edges.

—Jeanne Morton, 2019

* * * * *

"Andy, this is stunning," Sarah exclaimed as she gently unfolded the antique quilt. "Who is this Aunt Maddie, and why did she send this to you?"

"Aunt Maddie is the relative Caitlyn is living with in Nebraska, remember?"

"You mean the Miss Thompson I've heard so much about?"

Earlier in the year, Andy's daughter, Caitlyn, had done exhaustive computer searches, determined to find more family. As far as she and her father knew, their only relative was Andy's stepsister, who had been estranged from him for years and was now living in Indonesia with her current husband. With help from Sarah's computer-savvy husband, Charles, Caitlyn ultimately found a distant relative, a great-aunt in her nineties who was living in Nebraska.

After meeting Aunt Maddie, Caitlyn applied to and was accepted by the junior college near her aunt in Nebraska. Maddie was eager to have the young girl come live with her for the two years she'd be attending school.

"Yes, that's our aunt Maddie," Andy responded, "and Caitlyn is fascinated by her cottage, her life, her stories, and especially her quilts. I'm afraid she's not going to come back home, Sarah."

"Andy, that girl can't stay far from you. You know how much she loves you. She'll be home. I think this is a phase she's going through. She spent so many years without family to care for her, and now she's just enjoying having family."

"But you and Sophie have been family to her since she came to live with me. She even calls you Aunt Sarah. What more does she need?" Andy grumbled.

"And I love her like family, but she is searching for more. Just let her grow up in her own way, Andy. She's a very level-headed young woman."

Andy had unexpectedly become a father to a teenage girl and was still adjusting to the intricacies of the task.

The quilt was now carefully spread out on the bed in Sarah and Charles' guest room. "What do you know about the quilt?" Sarah asked, lightly lifting the worn edges and examining the few threadbare blocks.

"Not much. Aunt Maddie said it was made sometime in the late 1800s by her grandmother."

"Your great-grandmother?" Sarah marveled.

"I guess so. Never thought about it that way, but yeah, Maddie was my mother's sister, so they had the same mother and grandmother. Strange to think about, though," he added as he looked away. "My great-grandmother," he muttered.

Noticing Andy's discomfort, Sarah turned her attention to the quilt.

"This is a lovely scrap quilt, Andy, and in excellent condition considering its age. The fabrics are reminiscent of ones used during the Civil War period and on into the late nineteenth century, but I don't recognize the pattern. I'd like for Ruth to see it, but I'm hesitant to handle it too much." Ruth, the owner of the Running Stitches quilt shop, was the go-to person for all things quilt related in the area.

"Sarah, I know how you feel about antique quilts. I'd be perfectly willing for you to take it anywhere. I know you'll take good care of it. Just keep it here with you and take it to Ruth's shop whenever it's convenient."

Sarah started to object, but Andy spoke up. "Actually, it will be more convenient for me that way."

"Do you remember what happened the last time you asked me to take care of a quilt for you?"

They both burst out laughing. "I do remember," Andy recalled. "Your dog dragged it under your bed, and you had the police searching for an intruder!" They both continued to laugh as they reminisced.

As the two friends began to refold the quilt, Sarah asked in a more serious tone, "Andy, do you think there might be other relatives out there? Your great-grandmother might have had brothers and sisters who might have had children. You could discover cousins out there."

Andy looked doubtful. "Caitlyn and Charles did a pretty thorough search, Sarah. I doubt they missed anyone, but it wouldn't hurt to try again, I guess."

"May I ask a rather personal question, Andy?"

"Of course, Sarah," he responded, looking curious. "What is it?"

"Why didn't you know about this aunt? Maddie was your own mother's sister."

Andy sighed. "Mom died when I was very young, and my brother and I went to live with her mother. Granny told us many stories about our mother, but she never talked about her other daughter, Madeline. I was in my teens when I overheard the hushed tale about the daughter who ran off when she was seventeen, but to tell you the truth, I forgot all about it. To my knowledge, no one ever heard from her."

"That was Maddie?"

"Yes. I figure she must have run off about the time I was born. No one ever talked about her. If Mama had lived, I'd probably have heard about her, but Granny never brought it up."

"So this quilt is well over a hundred years old and a rare keepsake," Sarah said thoughtfully. "Now I definitely don't feel comfortable keeping it here, Andy."

"Okay, I'll take it home if you insist, but let me know when you want to take it to the quilt shop. I'll even go with you if that would make you more comfortable."

"Hey!" she exclaimed. "That gives me an idea. How would you like to bring the quilt to one of our quilt club meetings? The quilters would love seeing it and hearing its story. They could even give you ideas about caring for it."

"I guess I could as long as I don't have to talk or anything."

"Well," Sarah replied hesitantly, "I think talking would be an important part of sharing what you know about the quilt, but I would be with you. In fact, we could do the presentation together if you'd like."

"Me among all those women?" Andy questioned tentatively.

"Well, actually, we have one male member, but everyone would enjoy hearing about the quilt from its current owner."

"What could I say? I don't know anything about the quilt."

"Well, I could talk to Caitlyn and find out everything she and your aunt Maddie know about it. You could tell how you got it, and together we could talk about the quilt's history, and I could do some research and talk about the history of the pattern and the colors. How's that?"

"I suppose," he expressed reluctantly.

"It'll be fun," she replied.

"What will be fun?" Sarah's husband, Charles, asked as he entered the room. "And what's with that old ragged quilt?"

"This is no 'old ragged quilt,'" Sarah exploded. "This happens to be a valuable antique from the 1800s."

"I'm sorry," her husband responded contritely. "I had no idea." Charles hung his head in mock shame, but Sarah could see the playfulness in his eyes.

"Seriously, Charles, this quilt was made by one of Andy's relatives several generations ago." She went on to tell him about the presentation they had planned.

Charles simply shook his head in disbelief. "And you agreed to all this?" he asked, looking skeptically at his friend Andy.

"She can be very persuasive," Andy replied.

"That's an understatement," Charles muttered as he led the group into the kitchen for the spaghetti dinner he had promised earlier.

"I didn't know you were a cook," Andy commented as he watched Charles scoop the meatballs onto the bowl of pasta and sauce.

"Yes, I'm an expert at this. You should have seen me. I opened a can and a box, I boiled water, and I thawed frozen meatballs. I'm thinking of a second career as a chef."

"You should taste his chili con carne," Sarah teased. "He can make that with his eyes closed—just one can to open."

Chapter 2

"Charles, something is seriously wrong with my cell phone."

"What's it doing?"

"It's quacking."

"Quacking?" he asked with a frown.

"Yes, quacking."

Charles thought a moment and suddenly burst out laughing. "I had forgotten all about that," he said. "When I set up your new phone, I put a few notification sounds on it."

"I know. It plays classical music when I get a call. Actually, I'd like for it to just ring if you don't mind. You know, like a real telephone."

Charles started to point out that her smartphone was, in fact, a real telephone, but decided to keep that thought to himself. "Okay," he agreed. "I can do that."

"But that isn't the problem right now. Why is it quacking?"

"You told me you never wanted to send or receive text messages. Remember?"

"Yes, so?"

"You said you would just use your smartphone for making calls, but I went ahead and programmed a sound in case someone sent you a text message."

"Let me guess," she responded. "A duck?"

"Right!"

"And who's been texting me?"

"Let's take a look. Click right there."

"Oh, it was Caitlyn," Sarah exclaimed. "When did she send these messages?"

"See the notation above the message? This last one was sent yesterday at 3:14."

"Oh my. I hope she's okay." She quickly read the message. The message said:

[Caitlyn]

Do you text, Aunt Sarah?

"What do I do?" she asked Charles, handing him the phone.

He handed it back to her and showed her how to create a message.

"I don't know about this …" she said, frowning.

"Sarah, remember when we had the internet service that offered instant messaging?"

"Sure."

"Well, you wrote to me all the time, didn't you?"

"Sure, but that was on the computer."

"And this is on your cell phone. Same concept."

"Oh, I wish you'd told me about this sooner."

Charles sighed but didn't point out the obvious.

Sarah typed her response and looked at the Send button. She decided not to ask Charles any more questions since he seemed to be getting impatient with her. She tapped the Send button, and Caitlyn's response popped in moments later.

[Caitlyn]
Just leaving class. Will respond soon.

"Okay, she's going to get back to me. In the meantime, could you change the notification sound so Sophie will stop telling me I have a duck in my pocket?"

He took the phone and made a few quick adjustments.

"Thank you," she said as she put the phone back in her pocket.

"You are very welcome, my dear," he responded with a smile. "Sorry I got impatient."

"And why were you impatient with me, by the way?"

"Well, the fact is I've tried to tell you about texting many times, but you were never interested."

"Sorry, dear. Sometimes I feel like I'm on technology overload, but I'll try to be more receptive. I want to keep up."

"You don't have to worry about that, sweetie. You're way ahead of most people our age."

"Sophie and I were talking about the importance of learning new things, how it helps your brain function better during these senior years. I guess learning to use all these gadgets helps with that."

"I would certainly think so," Charles responded. "So, what are your plans today?"

"Tonight is quilt club, but this morning I'd like to go to the gym with you and then do some organizing in my sewing room. My stash is getting away from me, and I have several projects out on the worktable that I want to pack up."

"You aren't going to finish them?" he asked.

"Yes, eventually. But first I want to spend some time reorganizing my sewing room. Right now my shelves are a mishmash of yardage, pre-cuts, and scraps. I want to get some order in my stash so I know what I have."

Charles' eyes glazed over as they often did when Sarah talked about fabric or quilting.

As he was walking out of the kitchen, a sudden chirping sound came from Sarah's pocket, which caused her to drop the pan she was drying.

"There's a cricket in your pocket," Charles called over his shoulder as he disappeared down the hall. "Better see what it wants."

Sarah, muttering with amused annoyance, pulled the phone out of her pocket and was able to both read and respond to Caitlyn's message thanks to Charles' earlier instructions.

[Caitlyn]

I can talk now.

[Sarah]

I would prefer to do just that. I'll call you from my real phone. Is this a good time?

[Caitlyn]

Sure, Aunt Sarah.

detective, Charles, whom she ultimately married. "Life is good," she often said to anyone who would listen.

With a sigh, Sophie picked up her drink and a box of cookies and headed for Sarah's sewing room. Sarah followed with a bowl of grapes.

"He's with Irma," Sophie announced without looking back as they were leaving the kitchen.

"Irma?"

"Yes, Irma," Sophie responded impatiently. "You know. Irma. His wife."

"Wife?" Sarah exclaimed, stopping in the middle of the hallway.

"Okay, ex-wife."

In fact, Sarah had never heard the name Irma, nor did she know that Norman had an ex-wife. Norman was a partially retired event planner whom Sophie had met the previous year at the Community Center, where he was helping to arrange a celebration. They had begun dating and had settled into what Sarah thought was a comfortable relationship. Sophie had been reluctant to let the relationship develop into a more serious one, and Norman seemed willing to accept her boundaries, at least for now.

Sarah and Sophie assumed their usual spots in the sewing room: Sophie at the table Charles had set up for her Featherweight, and Sarah at the worktable he had built for her as part of the quilting station he had designed when they were first getting to know one another.

Since Sophie hadn't followed up on her earlier statement, Sarah figured that she genuinely didn't want to talk about Norman. Avoiding the subject, Sarah asked, "What are you going to be working on today?"

"Aren't you at all interested in knowing why he's with his ex-wife?" Sophie asked, sounding hurt and annoyed.

Sarah took a deep breath, knowing that she should carefully consider how she would respond. She'd never known her friend to be snarky like this, and she knew something was going on. *Anger? Frustration? Disappointment?* Sarah wondered.

"I think maybe you need to talk about this, Sophie," Sarah said gently. "I'm here, and you know I care about you. . . ."

Sophie's eyes began to tear up, but she fought to maintain control. "Oh, Sarah, I told you I didn't want to get involved with this man. I just wanted to have some fun—someone to go out to dinner with, a movie maybe—but then we started going to his cabin at the lake, and we were getting closer. I began to think, *Maybe this can work*, and then—*wham!* I let myself start to care, and what happens? His ex-wife shows up."

"Sophie, that doesn't necessarily mean . . ."

"Yes, it does. It means I pushed him away, and now he's going back to his ex-wife."

Sarah looked surprised. "He told you that?"

"Of course not," Sophie snapped, "but what else could it mean? He canceled our trip to the lake, and he hasn't called. He's there with her now. They're making plans to get back together. . . ."

"He told you that?" Sarah repeated, although more tentatively this time.

"No, he didn't," Sophie responded in a sharp tone that caused Emma and Barney to come running into the room. The dogs, tails and ears drooping, looked at their respective owners with wide-eyed alarm. Emma moved closer to Sophie's feet and searched her eyes.

Sophie gently stroked Emma's head but then stood and left the room. Moments later, Sarah heard the bathroom door being closed. She'd never seen her friend this upset. She usually joked with everyone, was always the life of the party, and never seemed to take anything seriously. Sophie was a jewel, and it pained Sarah to see her friend so troubled.

Emma looked up at Sarah with questioning eyes.

"She'll be right back, sweetie. Come with me to the kitchen, and I'll get you a biscuit." Barney wagged his tail, knowing that a treat was in store for him as well.

Sometime later, they heard the bathroom door being opened and Sophie's footsteps heading toward the sewing room.

"See?" Sarah mouthed to Emma as she led the dogs back to the sewing room to meet her friend.

The two women didn't mention their previous conversation as they worked on their projects. Sophie was making a wall hanging for her son, Timothy, and his wife.

"Do you think Martha will like it?" Sophie asked.

"She will love it, Sophie."

Sophie's son, Timothy, had returned to Middletown after retiring from his job at the company managing the Alaska pipeline. He met Sarah's daughter, Martha, and within a year they were married and living just a few blocks from the retirement village. The two mothers were ecstatic, and Sophie had announced that they were now related. "In fact, I think this makes us sisters," she had said.

"Martha will love the wall hanging," Sarah continued, "mostly because you made it, but also because you've chosen colors that perfectly complement the colors in their living room."

Sophie was accomplished with a needle but had resisted learning to quilt until she discovered the little sewing machine, which she later learned was a Singer Featherweight, in a secondhand store. Sarah spent many hours teaching her the basics of quilting, and Sophie was now quilting on her own.

When she decided to make a wall hanging for Timothy and Martha, Sarah helped her choose a pattern that was not too demanding. The pattern they found featured a group of daisies appliquéd on a pieced background. Sophie selected several neutral shades for the background and a soft green for the border. Sophie loved handwork and was very skilled at hand appliqué. She especially liked this particular pattern because the daisies spilled out onto the border. "I like things to feel free," Sophie had said.

"Will you help me figure out how to quilt this when I finish?" Sophie asked.

"Absolutely. I'm not particularly good at machine quilting, but this should be simple since you can do some outline quilting."

"What do you mean?" Sophie asked, looking uneasy.

"Don't worry, Sophie. We'll deal with that when you get there, but it won't be difficult. You and that little Featherweight of yours will have it done in no time."

The two worked quietly for a while, each woman lost in her own thoughts, until Sophie softly stated, "Maybe he's not even with her."

"What?" Sarah sounded surprised. "I thought you knew they were together."

"Not exactly. I was just surmising. I know she's in town."

"Sophie, Sophie," Sarah responded, shaking her head. "You are putting yourself through all this for nothing. Do you know how many times I've heard you say that people should never worry about imagined problems that might never occur?"

"I know. I know."

After another long silence, broken only by the hum of their sewing machines, Sophie said, "I've had an idea that I want to run past you."

Oh my, Sarah thought, thinking that her friend was still obsessing about Norman and Irma.

"Yes?" she responded tentatively.

"Well, I saw this metal hanger for small wall hangings. It looked sort of like a regular wire hanger but with some curlicues here and there that made it fancier. There was one that was just wide enough for this wall hanging."

"That sounds nice," Sarah responded, pleased that she had been wrong about the topic. "Are you thinking of buying it for them?"

"More than that. I'm thinking about giving it to Tim and Martha along with this wall hanging, but then I'll continue to make wall hangings this size so they can change them with the seasons. What do you think?"

"I think that's a fantastic idea, Sophie," Sarah responded enthusiastically.

"It's hard to find presents for adults who already have everything they want," Sophie continued, "and I thought this would be a nice solution to gift giving."

"I love the idea," Sarah responded.

They talked about various gift ideas, and no mention was made of Norman or Irma the rest of the afternoon. At the end of their sew-in, Sophie packed up her materials and headed toward the front door. "Come on, Emma. Time to go home."

Emma, her furry friend, had been curled up under the futon with her head resting on Barney's back. She slithered out and stretched before following her favorite human toward the door.

As Sophie was walking toward her car, she called out over her shoulder, "Well, I guess I'll just ask him about Irma."

"Good idea, Sophie."

"She's back," Sarah murmured with a smile as she led Barney back into the house.

Chapter 4

"Did you gals have a good time?" Charles asked when he returned from the gym.

"We got a lot of sewing done. Sophie was upset about Norman, but otherwise it was a productive day."

"What's going on with Norman?"

Sarah told her husband what little she knew and then said, "But she has had a great idea for gift giving, and I thought I might also do it for Jason and Jenny. Sophie found this metal quilt hanger and is planning to make a variety of wall quilts for …"

As usual when she was describing a quilt project, Charles' eyes began to glaze over. "Never mind," she added. "I'll show you when I finish it."

"Sounds great," he responded, as if he now knew all about the project. "By the way, have you spoken to Andy about the presentation?"

"Andy and I are taking the dogs to the dog park tomorrow, so we'll talk about it there."

"Why the dog park?" Charles asked.

"Andy suggested it. I think he wants company when he walks little Sabrina. He hasn't walked her over there since Caitlyn left, and he wanted company the first time."

"That seems strange. Did Andy say why? He's a pretty tough guy."

"And that may be exactly the reason," Sarah responded. "That little miniature dachshund is a very prissy little girl. He may be embarrassed to be seen with her."

"You may be right," Charles said with a chuckle. "I'm not sure I could do it. I'm glad we have this scruffy old mutt," he added as he reached down and lovingly scratched Barney's head. Barney looked up, returning the love with his eyes.

"How old do you suppose this little guy is now?" Charles asked.

"The rescue folks said they thought he was five or six when they got him, but they couldn't be sure because of his condition. That was more than five years ago, so he's probably ten or eleven."

A look of sadness crossed Charles' face as he again reached down to pet Barney.

"He's in pretty good health, though," Sarah added. "At least that's what the vet said before he retired."

"He hasn't been seen for a while," Charles responded thoughtfully.

"True, but except for these signs of old age he seems fine. I order his joint medication, and it doesn't require a prescription. I think he'll be with us for a very long time," Sarah concluded, demonstrating her usual positive outlook. Then she thought, *Sophie would have said I'm being Pollyanna again, if she'd been listening to the conversation.*

As Sarah was leaving the kitchen, she bent down and hugged her dog. Charles saw a trace of moisture in her eyes but remained silent.

* * * * *

As it turned out, Sarah and Andy didn't accomplish much planning at the dog park. Caitlyn's little dachshund, Sabrina, took a fancy to a very regal miniature pinscher. "Are you sure that's a pinscher?" Sarah asked. "It looks like a little Doberman."

"It's a pinscher, for sure," Andy insisted. "That dog and Sabrina have some genes in common."

"I didn't know you knew about dogs," Sarah replied, looking surprised.

"I don't. I only know what Caitlyn told me when she was reading about her little dachshund. It seems the dachshund, the Italian greyhound, and the shorthaired German pinscher were involved in the creation of the miniature pinscher."

"Amazing," Sarah said with a frown. "Creating dogs. Somehow that doesn't seem right."

"It may not be right," Andy responded, "but it's becoming popular. I saw an ad for a goldendoodle online this morning—a cross between a poodle and a golden retriever."

"Yes, I think they're calling those designer dogs. Becky in the quilt club just got a pomapoo, a combination of a Pomeranian and a poodle, but she was looking at a labradoodle first."

"That must be a combination of a Labrador and a poodle. They seem to like using poodles for many of these new designs," Andy added.

They sat quietly for a while, watching the dogs performing the rituals understood by all members of their species. They sniffed their greetings and signaled their invitations to play, while some declared their desire to be left alone.

"Did you know that some dogs can detect the presence of cancer?" Andy asked. "And some can predict when an epileptic seizure is coming on."

"I've read that," Sarah replied. "I've also read that they have many of the same emotions we have, like jealousy and grief. But it's believed that they don't feel guilt."

"That would be nice. I'm always feeling guilty about something," Andy replied. "I try not to, but I get caught up in it."

"Maybe that's a good thing. Perhaps it keeps us on the right path, at least some of the time," Sarah responded.

A few more dogs joined in the activities until one lost his temper, and Andy felt he should remove Sabrina for her protection. Barney followed them to the gate reluctantly and waited for Sarah to attach his leash. He loved his time in the park, and his tail and ears drooped as he headed toward home.

"Can you come to my house tomorrow, Sarah? We need peace and quiet for this planning exercise, and I need notes about what I'm supposed to say."

"Okay, that sounds like a good plan. How's 10:00?"

"Just right," Andy replied. "Tomorrow is my day to sleep in."

On her way home, Sarah decided to stop at Sophie's. She'd been wondering what had happened between her friend and Norman but didn't want to ask. The two women sat down at the kitchen table, where Sophie had poured iced tea and set out the cookie jar along with a couple of napkins. "Help yourself," she said.

As if reading her friend's mind, Sophie added, "So I asked Norman about Irma."

"And?"

"He said, 'Yes, she's in town,' and that's all he said. I didn't know what else to ask, so I let it drop. What do you think that means?"

"Do you want me to tell you what my best friend, Sophie Ward, told me once?"

"I suppose," Sophie responded skeptically, while silently vowing to stop giving advice since it seemed always to come back to bite her. "What did I tell you?"

"You told me not to try to figure out what people mean or what people are thinking. You said I should either ask them what they mean or drop it. You also said that if I try to figure it out without asking, I'll probably get it wrong."

"So I should ask him, or I should drop it," Sophie pondered. "I think I'll drop it."

"Okay," Sarah responded reluctantly.

"At least for now," Sophie muttered.

* * * * *

"Sarah, can you come over right away?" Sophie sobbed on the phone early the next morning.

"Oh, Sophie, have you fallen?"

"It's nothing like that, Sarah, but I need you. Don't bring Charles. This is a female thing."

"I'm going to Sophie's," Sarah called over her shoulder as she pulled on her coat and snapped Barney's leash onto his harness. She decided it would be just as fast to walk and not spend time explaining to Barney why they weren't going for a walk.

"What is it?" she asked immediately upon arriving at her friend's house.

"Take your coat off and come into the kitchen. This conversation requires sugar."

Once they were settled at Sophie's table, each with a slice of warmed apple pie, Sophie announced, "Norman is with Irma in Kentucky at his cabin."

"You know this for sure this time?"

"Yes. I called him, and I heard voices in the background. Lots of voices, for that matter, and I asked him where he was. He said he was at the cabin."

"And all the voices in the background?" Sarah asked. "Who else was there?"

"His entire family."

"What did he say about it?"

"He said they had a family issue to discuss, and he'd explain when he came back later this week."

Sarah, for the second time that day, didn't know what to say. She could tell her friend was on edge, and she wanted to be supportive, but she didn't think this family get-together necessarily meant that Sophie was being pushed out of Norman's life.

"It could be anything. . . ." Sarah said cautiously.

"Sure, it could be," Sophie responded, "and the most likely thing would be they are meeting with their children to tell them they are getting back together."

"Sophie, I know you don't want to hear this. . . ."

"So must I?"

"Yes, you must. You know Norman, and I think I know him too. He's an honorable man. And yes, he might decide to go back to Irma, but he would never do that without telling you first. He cares too much for you to hurt you like that."

"I would have thought so," Sophie mumbled.

"I would like to tell you to trust what you know about the man, but I know that statement would only upset you."

"I think you just did tell me that," Sophie responded with a half-smile. "And I know you're right. I'll wait until he's ready to talk. But in the meantime, I'm preparing myself to lose him. I won't be any worse off than I was before I met him."

"True," Sarah responded, knowing that wasn't entirely true.

"Except, of course," Sophie added, "I didn't have a broken heart back then."

Sarah stood and walked around the table. "I know you don't like hugs, but I need one right now, so you'll have to 'suck it up' as Andy says." The two women embraced, and Sophie allowed a few tears to find their way down her cheek.

"Sorry to bring you out in the cold," Sophie said as Sarah was returning to her chair.

"No problem. I had to come out anyway to get a piece of this apple pie."

Chapter 5

"So, where do we start?" Andy asked. "And remember, I don't want to do much talking."

"Do you want me to start? I could introduce you and tell the group why you are there."

"Why am I there?" Andy asked anxiously.

"Andy, you've got to relax. Please believe me when I tell you that once you meet these ladies and see what a fun, relaxed group it is, you'll be fine. I have an idea. Instead of starting right out today trying to plan the presentation, let's just drink our coffee and talk a bit." *I've got to get this man to relax*, Sarah told herself.

"Okay, what shall we talk about?" Andy asked compliantly.

"I'd like to know more about your family."

"There's not much to tell, but okay. What would you like to know?"

"You told me that you and your brother lived with your grandmother after your mother died. But what about your sister? I remember a younger woman—Brenda, I think—who came to your funeral, or what we thought was your funeral. Anyway, what about her? How does she fit in?"

"Actually, she doesn't fit in at all, and I have no idea why she came to my so-called funeral. After my mother died, Dad remarried—not right away, but sooner than my grandmother thought was right. I remember all the fuss she made. George and I just listened and didn't really understand. In retrospect, I suppose this woman was looking for a father for her little girl. But once they married, that was the end of our contact with him. He died long ago, and his wife and her daughter aren't family by any definition. I know some families can include stepbrothers and stepsisters, but it's something that develops, and with us nothing ever developed. Once our mother died, our father forgot we existed."

"So, she was a stepsister," Sarah pondered. "And George? I know he's passed away. . . ."

"That's putting it mildly," Andy sputtered sarcastically. A few years earlier, Andy had had an altercation with his brother and ended up in prison for a short time.

"So, tell me about you and George when you were living with your grandmother," Sarah asked, changing the subject somewhat. "I know you were twins, and I've heard there's no closer relationship than that, yet you never mention him when you talk about your childhood."

"George was my twin for sure, and I've heard all those things about twins, but we couldn't have been any different if we'd each been born to entirely different parents. George was always in trouble. Most of his life was spent in lockup: first juvie, then prison."

"And you were different."

"Not so different, I guess. I just acted out in a different way. Remember I told you when I first met you that I was in Alcoholics Anonymous?"

"I remember," Sarah replied.

"Well, that was the end of a long period of drunkenness and behavior I'd rather forget. But I must admit, if I hadn't been inebriated most of the time back then, I never would have hooked up with that woman, and my sweet Caitlyn would never have been conceived. It all worked out."

"You made it work out, Andy."

"I guess," he said with his usual humility. "Anyway, why are we talking about all this? We have a presentation to plan."

Sarah smiled as he spread out the quilt.

"It's a pretty sad-looking thing," Andy said, looking discouraged.

"It's exactly what it should be. It holds the history of all the people who have used it for warmth, for spreading on the ground for picnics and stargazing and …"

"Okay, I get it. It's lived life to the fullest," Andy said with a chuckle. "So, what are we going to say about this ragged quilt?"

"You're going to tell how you came by it, and I hope you'll read the note Maddie included in the package. Do you have it handy?"

"I do." Andy went to his desk and picked up an envelope, which he opened, and began reading.

To my nephew, Andrew Burgess,

You and Caitlyn are the only ones left to carry on our family name. I regret all the years we could have been involved in each other's lives. I accept full responsibility for that loss. I was young and crazy when I took off with that boy. I was seventeen, jealous of all the attention my sister was getting because of her upcoming marriage, and I just ran off with the one boy my parents disliked the most. I was trying to hurt them, but I hurt myself in the process.

None of that explains why I never contacted the family again. Shame, maybe? Perhaps when you come to visit me, we can talk about those lost years.

What I also regret is taking this quilt when I left. I knew how much my mother loved it and that it was the only remembrance she had of her own family. I was very young, but I remember listening to her talk about her grandmother making the quilt in the late 1800s. It was a valued keepsake, and I took it to hurt my mother. I was a terrible child and will never forgive myself, but I hope you can forgive me.

I'm in my nineties, as you know, and I want you and Caitlyn to have this quilt and give it the love and care it deserves. Please do that for our family.

With affection,

Madeline Thompson, your Aunt Maddie

"That's a very touching story, Andy. It sounds like your aunt Maddie suffered a lifetime of regret."

"I agree. And I'm sure Maddie realizes this is her last chance to make amends—not to the people she hurt, but at least to the family. I'm glad we found her when we did and that she and Caitlyn are having a wonderful time together."

"Do you plan to visit as she said?"

"Absolutely. I hope to spend Christmas with them."

"I don't know how much you want to share with the group, Andy. This is pretty private stuff. Maybe you wouldn't want to read the letter to them."

"No, you're wrong. I want to share the story. It's not just Aunt Maddie's story. It's this quilt's story, and it deserves to be told."

Sarah smiled, appreciating her friend's sensitive nature. "Then I think we just prepared your presentation."

"Really?"

"Sure," Sarah responded. "This letter will lead to conversation, and I'm sure Ruth and Delores, along with several of the other older quilters, can tell us a great deal about the actual quilt. We're finished."

Andy took a deep sigh and said, "I hope you're right."

Chapter 6

Several mornings later, as Sarah and Charles were peacefully attending to their morning routines, Sarah heard her husband answer the phone in the kitchen. She assumed it was for her, but when he didn't call her, she went back to making the bed and straightening their room. Sarah glanced outside and saw that the rain had started up again. She opened the French doors and stepped out onto the heated porch, which they now called their sunroom, and enjoyed the peacefulness of the gentle rainfall.

"Sophie's on the line," Charles announced sometime later, appearing at their bedroom door.

"I didn't hear it ring," she responded, but then she remembered. "Oh yes, I did, but that was a long time ago. Have you been talking to her all this time?" she asked as she took the phone from her pajama-clad husband.

"She needed a man's view on something."

Sarah didn't need to ask about the topic, knowing that it had to do with what had been on her friend's mind for some time now. "Norman again?" she whispered with her hand over the mouthpiece.

"Norman," he responded, shaking his head. "He's on his way back from the cabin, and … oh, let her tell you. She's waiting."

"Hi, Sophie. It sounds like there's been a development."

"There has. Norman is on his way home and wants to talk to me. I'm so nervous I can barely eat these donuts."

"How about you come over here, and you can catch me up on what's happening."

"I already arranged for both of you to come to my house. I hope you don't mind. Charles said it was fine with him."

"Whatever you and Charles worked out is certainly fine with me, but what's going on?"

"Norman wants to talk, and I think I'm going to need support after he drops his bombshell. Is it okay?" she asked in a pleading tone.

"Of course, Sophie. I think that's a good idea. When will he be there?"

"He said he'd get here about eleven. Can you get here by then?"

Sarah looked at the clock and saw that it was already ten. "Okay, I'll get dressed now, and we'll head on over."

"Come as soon as you can, okay?" Sophie asked. "And bring Barney along to keep Emma company."

"He's holding his leash in his mouth already. We'll be right over."

"This will be interesting," Charles mused as he began to dress.

* * * * *

"Would you get the door, Charles?" Sophie asked. "I'm just too nervous."

"Sure," Charles responded as he got up from the table where the three had been drinking coffee and eating the last of Sophie's donuts. Both dogs jumped up and followed him.

"We should have saved a donut or two for Norman," Sophie said, but then corrected herself with, "but after he says his piece, he may not deserve donuts."

"I'll throw the box away, and we can just take coffee into the living room," Sarah suggested.

They both heard Charles greeting Norman, and Sarah called out for them to make themselves comfortable in the living room. "We're bringing coffee."

"I'm trembling," Sophie whispered. "Why am I so nervous? I know what he's going to say."

"Let's go, Sophie. After we say hello, Charles and I will come back into the kitchen."

"No!" Sophie demanded. "I want you with me. I can't do this alone."

Sarah sighed, hoping Norman wouldn't object. The two women were each carrying two mugs of coffee. Sarah handed one to Charles, which forced Sophie to be the one to serve Norman. Sophie shot Sarah a disapproving look before frostily saying, "Hello, Norman. I hope you had a safe trip in this rain."

"I did fine, thank you," he responded, sounding unnaturally formal.

"Sarah," Charles began as he stood. "Let's give these two some privacy."

"No!" Sophie exclaimed.

"That's not necessary," Norman agreed. "What I have to say you will all know very soon. And besides, we're all friends here."

"Humph," Sophie muttered.

Charles looked to Sarah for guidance, and she nodded toward the couch for him to join her.

Everyone was quiet for a few moments as they sipped their coffee. The dogs, sensing the tension, had refused to go outside and had curled up together on Emma's living room quilt.

Finally, Norman took a deep breath and turned to Sophie, although she continued to avoid looking directly at him. "Honey," he began. "I'm so sorry I didn't confide in you. I didn't know what to say to you about Irma being in town, so I took the easy way out and didn't say anything. When Irma called and asked me to get the kids together at the cabin, I had no idea what was going on. She just said she needed to speak to everyone at once. The cabin was a logical place to meet since it's centrally located. Well, you know that since you and I picked it out for that very reason."

"Okay, I can understand that, but why did you need to be there?"

"Well, we had an amicable divorce, and to tell you the truth, I was curious. I was afraid she was critically ill. She had cancer a few years before we separated, and I thought maybe it had come back. Anyway, if she was going to tell the kids something like that, I wanted to be there for them. Anyway, it's my cabin. Actually, mine and Sophie's," he added, catching Sophie's eye for the first time.

Sophie dropped her eyes immediately and asked, "So what was it all about?" She waited for the other shoe to drop, still certain that their relationship was coming to an end.

"Well, in fact, it was something fantastic. A very wealthy aunt of hers had died...."

"That doesn't sound too fantastic, especially for the aunt," Sophie responded glibly.

"Oh, that's not the fantastic part," Norman explained. "Irma hardly knew this aunt, but she was the aunt's closest living relative. Anyway, this aunt left Irma her entire fortune, including the hundred-year-old family mansion, which Irma immediately sold."

"So now she's very rich," Sophie noted, wondering if that was the reason Norman was going back to her.

Norman continued, "So she wants to take the entire family—the kids, the grandkids, and our one great-grandchild—on an Alaskan cruise."

So there it is, Sophie thought. *The other shoe.*

"That's very generous," Sophie responded coolly. "And when do you leave?"

"When do I leave?" Norman responded incredulously. "Sophie, we're divorced. I'm not going. When I said we divorced amicably, I certainly didn't mean we vacation together!"

Sophie took a deep breath, beginning to suspect that she might have been wrong about what was going on. She glanced at Sarah, who nodded reassuringly. Charles winked at her as if to say, "Everything is okay."

"And that's not the best part," Norman added. "She's setting up large trust funds for all the youngsters and had generous checks for all the parents."

"I'm sorry, Norman."

"Sorry?" Norman looked baffled. "I don't understand. What are you sorry about? I'm the one ..."

"I'm sorry for not trusting you and for all the terrible things I thought and said. I behaved very badly. I'm ashamed. I should have known better."

"You didn't say any terrible things to me...." Norman stammered.

"You're lucky I didn't," Sophie said with a chuckle, "but Sarah and Charles sure got an earful."

Everyone laughed as Sophie broke the tension.

"Do you think you'll be able to forgive me?" Norman asked, walking over and taking her hand.

"There's nothing to forgive, Norman. You're a good man, and you've always been trustworthy. I put myself through all this because I didn't believe in you, and I should have." Norman raised Sophie's hand to his lips and gently kissed it.

As they continued to look into each other's eyes, Sarah knew it was going to work out for her friend, who was clearly in love with this man.

"So, you're still my girl?" Norman asked with his head tilted and a cockeyed grin on his face.

"Sure," she answered, giggling. "I'm still your *girl*."

"So let's all go celebrate. How about lunch at our favorite Italian restaurant?"

"Sounds like an excellent idea," Charles responded.

"It's fine with me, but what are we celebrating?" Sophie asked.

"We're celebrating the fact that my kids will never again be asking me for a penny."

Chapter 7

"Well, are you ready?" Sarah asked enthusiastically as she climbed into Andy's van.

"As ready as I'll ever be," he responded without enthusiasm. His tone conveyed a feeling of dread.

"Come on, Andy. This will be fun. Sophie will be there, and I'm sure you'll enjoy the quilters. And I know they'll love you and your quilt."

"We'll see," he muttered.

To take her friend's attention off his concern about the meeting, Sarah launched into an account of her most recent experience at the nursing home with their mutual friend Sophie. "You should have seen her, Andy. She decided she could ride the recumbent bike when the patient she was visiting insisted that she accompany him to his physical therapy session." Andy began to smile as he listened. "So she lowered herself onto it and was able to pedal for a while. That's when she called me at home to come over right away."

"Why?" Andy asked, now engrossed in her story.

"She couldn't get up and didn't want to tell anyone. She told me later that she had hoped to keep pedaling until I got there."

"Surely there were people who could have helped her...."

"Sure, but remember? She was pretending everything was fine."

"And were you able to help her?"

"By the time I got there, the staff had realized her predicament and had helped her up. She was sitting on the weight bench eyeing the weights. 'Forget it,' I told her and took her straight home."

Andy had forgotten his worries and was still chuckling when they walked into Running Stitches.

"You must be Andy," the woman standing by the register said. She quickly walked around the counter and offered her hand. "I'm Ruth Weaver, and this is my sister, Anna. We're so happy you are joining us tonight."

"Yes, I'm Andy Burgess, and I'm happy to be here," Andy replied. "Well, that's not entirely true," he added. "I'm actually terrified. I don't know how I let Sarah talk me into this."

But Ruth knew better because this gentle man had kind eyes and a caring smile.

"Well, you can relax here. We're quilters—the nicest folks in the world, you may have heard—and we've been eagerly awaiting your arrival. Quilters," she suddenly called out to the group surrounding the coffee and dessert table, "come meet Caitlyn's father and tonight's presenter."

Introductions were made all around until Andy's eyes were spinning. "I'll never remember everyone's name, but I can hardly wait to call Caitlyn and tell her I met all you folks."

After a half hour spent enjoying the variety of cakes and conversation, primarily about Caitlyn and how much she was missed, Ruth asked everyone to find a seat, and she led

Andy and Sarah to their seats. Before the meeting, Ruth had pushed two tables together to make a large square and placed most of the chairs around three sides, with just Andy and Sarah at the head.

"I arranged the table this way," she said, "so we'd have a large tabletop space for displaying the quilt without having to handle it directly." Everyone nodded, knowing that Ruth was actually instructing them to keep their hands off the quilt. "Sarah, would you like to introduce our speaker?"

"You've all met Andy by now," Sarah began. "If you haven't, this is Andy Burgess, Caitlyn's father and a dear friend of mine and Sophie's. Andy received a gift from a family member, which he'd like to share with you tonight. Andy would also like to learn more about his quilt, so as you're looking at it, please share what you might know about the pattern, the fabrics … anything.

"We'll begin with Andy telling you how he came to receive this quilt, but we won't spread it out until after he does that so you won't be distracted." Sarah had learned this the hard way. She often taught classes at the quilt shop and discovered that if she passed out the instructions or pictures of their projects before speaking, no one was able to listen because of their eagerness to see what they would be doing.

"Andy?" she said, turning to her friend. His hands were trembling, but he began talking, often looking at Sophie for support. He told a bit about Caitlyn's search for a relative and shared some of what he had told Sarah the previous week. She was surprised at first but then realized he needed to say those things to put the letter in context.

He then unfolded the letter and read it to the group. Once his voice cracked with emotion, but he was able to speak through it. When he reached the end of the letter, the room remained silent. Sarah noticed that several women had tears in their eyes. Suddenly everyone applauded.

Andy took a deep breath and smiled. “Thank you,” he said, “and my aunt Maddie thanks you. She led a life of regret, and Caitlyn and I are hoping to help make the rest of her years happy ones.”

“Now, let’s take a look at that quilt,” Ruth announced excitedly. She helped Sarah and Andy spread the quilt out on the table. It just fit, with everyone having a part of the quilt near them.

“It’s damaged,” Frank grumbled, looking disappointed.

“It’s well over a hundred years old, Frank,” Ruth said. “Probably more like 120 years old. And remember what we talked about the last time we had a very old quilt? Its flaws only tell us it has been used and loved over the years. It tells us something about its history.”

“And about its life,” Frank added, remembering what Ruth had told him. Frank was somewhat limited developmentally, but he had been very successful with simple quilting projects. He had been a part of the group for several years, frequently making things for his grandmother.

“I don’t recognize the pattern, but it looks very complicated, with points going out here and there,” Becky said as she studied the pattern.

Ruth and Delores, the two most experienced quilters, simply smiled and stepped away from the table. Sophie realized that the two women already understood the pattern, but she was determined to figure it out for herself. She moved closer to the quilt and started in one corner, looking for the repetition, just as Delores had shown her in class.

"What are you doing?" Sarah asked.

"I'm looking for that one block that will lead me to the design of the quilt."

Others joined her, and Kimberly remarked, "There are certainly lots of four-patches."

Her sister, Christina, immediately added, "And lots of snowball corners."

"What's a snowball corner?" Sophie asked, abandoning her investigation for the moment.

"It's when you add a half-square triangle to the corner of a square block. If you put one on all four corners, the block appears to be round. I guess that's why it's called a snowball corner, but in this quilt, the half-square triangles are only on two of the corners."

"Two opposite corners," Allison added, "but sometimes the top one is on the right corner, and sometimes it's on the left corner. I'm totally confused. This looks like a very difficult quilt."

"We aren't going to be making it, are we?" Becky cried.

"No, we're just analyzing how it was made right now," Ruth responded. "But if you want to …"

"*No!*" Becky squealed. "I'm having enough trouble with the simple Irish Chain I'm working on."

"Well, I can't make sense of it," Sophie finally admitted, returning to her seat. "But I love it."

"Okay," Ruth responded. "Are you ready to hear how simple this quilt is to make?"

"You bet," Allison replied.

"This quilt has two blocks and only two blocks. One is a simple four-patch, and the other is a square with two snowball corners."

"But they go in all different directions," Becky responded.

"No, look more carefully. It's all in the placement. Divide the quilt into fourths right through the middle and look again. The bottom left quarter is the reverse placement of the bottom right. And look at the top. They are also reversed in the other direction."

"I see it," Sophie cried as she jumped out of her chair. "The top left quarter is exactly like the bottom right quarter!"

"You're right, Sophie," Delores responded with a proud smile. Sophie had been one of her favorite students.

"Wait a minute," Becky announced. "You said there were only two blocks: a four-patch and the square with snowball corners, but I see a sixteen-patch block right in the middle!"

"Look again," Ruth said patiently. "Remember the four quarters? That's where they meet in the middle. Each quarter is contributing one four-patch to that block you're looking at."

"Of course," Becky agreed. "It really is pretty straightforward. Like you said, 'It's all in the placement.' "

As the group continued to examine the quilt, someone said, "This was completely stitched by hand, wasn't it?"

"It was hand pieced and hand quilted," Ruth responded. "Just look at these perfect stitches."

"Yes," Sarah said, "but look at these stitches over here. They are irregular and look like they were made by an inexperienced person."

"Several people must have worked on this quilt, and perhaps those stitches were made by a younger person, or someone who was just learning," Ruth suggested.

"How do you think this quilt should be repaired?" Kimberly asked, looking at the blocks with disintegrating fabric.

"Unless Andy wants to keep it in its original condition, I'd suggest finding compatible fabric and appliquéing over the damaged blocks," Delores responded. "Actually, there aren't that many—mostly just along this fold line."

"What do you think you'll do about those, Andy?"

"I have no idea what you ladies are talking about," Andy announced as he stood up, "but I'm getting another cup of coffee." Everyone laughed as Sarah and Ruth began to carefully fold the quilt so they could return it to Andy's duffel bag.

"I love doing this," Allison said. "I've learned so much tonight. I'll bet a few of us have old quilts at home. Why don't we bring them in and talk about them as well?"

"I don't have any," Becky replied, "but I'd love looking at the others."

"How many people have an antique quilt at home?" Allison queried.

"How old does it have to be to be an antique?" Peggy asked. "I have old quilts from the 1960s and 70s, but they probably aren't antique, are they?"

"A general rule of thumb," Ruth explained, "seems to be that items over one hundred years old are antique and over fifty years are vintage, but lots of people don't follow that rule. As far as I'm concerned, I'd be happy to see old quilts of any age."

"I agree," said Delores. "So let's repeat the question. Who has an old quilt to share with the group?"

Almost everyone in the room raised their hands.

"My granny has a bunch of them in the attic," Frank announced. "She'd let me bring some."

"I have some, too," Myrtle offered. "They're in terrible shape. I kept meaning to repair them, but I never did." Myrtle, now in her mid-eighties, had recently returned to the group after a stay in the nursing home's rehabilitation center following hip surgery. She was now walking without her cane and was eager to get back to quilting.

"Shall we plan on bringing a few to our next meeting to look at?" Ruth asked.

"Wait a minute," Sarah interrupted. "Sophie, would you tell the group about your idea?"

Sophie struggled to stand, although it wasn't necessary. No one else was standing, but Sophie, being short, preferred to stand when she spoke to the entire group. Ruth had given up suggesting that she remain seated.

"I had this idea about us having a quilt show and displaying all our old quilts. I talked to Sarah about it, and we thought it would be fun. We could even charge a small fee and earn money for charity projects in the future."

"How many old quilts do we have among us?" Ruth asked, and members began calling out numbers.

"Okay, I didn't write those down, but it sounds like if I add the quilts I have at home, we'd have at least a couple dozen, probably more with what Frank's grandmother has. That would be enough. We could include a write-up about each one. People would be interested in knowing something about each quilt."

"Where would we have it?" Delores asked. "This shop is too small."

"We thought of that," Sophie added. "We could probably have it at the Cunningham Village Community Center. They're always doing things like that—art exhibits, book signings. We might have to share some of the proceeds with them."

Excitement was growing around the table. "We'd all need to be there, making sure no one was touching the quilts," Christina added.

"That part would be fun. We would be 'white-glove ladies.' "

"What about security?" one member asked.

"I could probably help with that," Andy offered. Everyone turned to look at him. After returning with his coffee and a couple of pastries, he had been sitting quietly, just listening, but with interest.

"I'm sure my husband would be happy to help," Sarah offered, knowing her retired detective husband would jump at the opportunity.

"I hate to interrupt this lively discussion, but we've run way over time," Ruth interjected, "and I'm sure your families are wondering where you are. I'll look into this idea and report back at our next meeting. I think we may have come up with an exciting project. I'll check with the Community Center tomorrow and see what they think of the idea."

"How do you think it went?" Andy asked as they were driving home.

"I think the club members loved your presentation and that incredible quilt. Thank you for doing this, Andy. I know it was stressful for you."

"Much more than it should have been," he responded. "You were right all along. By the way, why didn't Sophie ride with us?"

"She wanted Norman to bring her and pick her up. They went out to dinner before the meeting …" she began.

"… and he's staying over," Andy finished.

"Not our business, Andy."

"Just saying …"

"Not our business," she repeated firmly.

Chapter 8

"Miss Thompson, this is Sarah Miller calling. I'm ..."

"Sarah, I know who you are, and I'm so glad you called. Caitlyn talks about you all the time. I've wanted to call, but I wasn't sure if it would be appropriate. ..."

"I wish you had, Miss Thompson. You and I have a great deal in common. We both love that young girl."

"Isn't she remarkable?" Caitlyn's great-aunt replied enthusiastically.

The two women talked for twenty minutes or so, getting to know one another. "You know, Caitlyn looks just like my sister, Cora Lee, did at that age."

"Andy's mother, right?"

"Yes, Andy's mother. I don't know if you know the whole story, but I left home when I was seventeen and never saw any of the family again."

"I'm so sorry," Sarah responded tenderly. "That must have been hard."

"I didn't realize how hard it was at the time. I was a rebellious, angry teenager long before it was in vogue! By the time I started growing up and realizing what I had done, my family was essentially gone. Cora Lee died shortly after her twins, Andy and George, were born. Our mother passed away not long after that."

"Oh, I thought the boys went to live with her," Sarah responded.

"They went to live with their other grandmother. She lived in the next county, and you probably know about their father? Cora Lee's husband?"

"Very little. Andy doesn't talk about his father much."

"Well, he married a woman with a child, and they pretty much dropped out of sight. Those boys grew up without parents. Andy turned out fine, but his brother, George, paid the price. I understand he spent most of his life in and out of prison."

"Well, I can vouch for Andy. He's a good man, kind and caring, and the best friend a person could have. And he's done a fantastic job with his daughter."

"He sure has," Maddie responded. "Caitlyn is a fine young woman."

"So, Miss Thompson, I wanted to ask you a few questions about the quilt. You know, we're having a local quilt show featuring antique quilts, and Andy asked me to write the history of your quilt for the exhibit."

"Well, first of all, please call me Maddie. You are practically family, and it feels good to have some family in my life for the first time in all these years. I want to tell you about the quilt, but most of what I'm going to say can't go on the sign. It's too personal."

"You will be able to approve what we write before it's displayed, but I'd love to hear whatever you're willing to tell me. It's such a lovely quilt—all hand pieced and quilted. Do you know if it had a name? There was no label."

"It was made by my grandmother, Minnie Evans. I don't know exactly when, but I do know she made it for her daughter, Gloria, my mother. I'm sure of that because Mama always called it her 'wedding quilt.' She was married sometime in the late 1800s, so that tells us when it must have been made."

"That means the quilt is at least 120 years old!" Sarah exclaimed.

"I suppose so. It was on my parents' bed throughout my entire childhood. Mama treated it with such loving care. It was probably her most precious possession and the only quilt that survived in our family from that generation."

"She must have treasured it," Sarah said before remembering that Maddie had taken it when she ran off. She was sorry she had said it, but it was too late to take it back.

"She did, and I knew that. Like I said in my note to Andy, I was a rebellious child, jealous of my sister, who I felt was favored by my parents. When I look back on it all today, I can see why I might have thought that. Cora Lee was a good daughter and never got into trouble. I was always in trouble, and you know how kids can interpret things. It seemed to me they loved her more since they didn't punish her as often, when, in fact, I deserved every punishment I received."

Sarah sighed silently, feeling sad for that little girl of long ago.

"Anyway, I ran off mainly to ruin Cora Lee's wedding and to defy my parents. At the last minute, I yanked the quilt off Mama's bed and took it with me. I was immediately sorry about that."

"Where did you go? You were so young."

"The farmer's son up the road was taking off for a job on a cattle ranch in Oklahoma, and I went with him. That turned out to be a disaster. I stayed with Joe for a few years, but they were rough years. He turned into a mean drunk and kept me with him until I finally had a chance to run off. I headed back home, but nobody was left by then except the folks on a neighboring farm. They gave me temporary work and helped me get into nursing school, which had been a dream of mine. I ended up working at the local hospital until I retired. It was a good life, but a lonely one."

"You never married?"

"My experience with Joe made me very cautious ... too cautious, I guess. I never married, but I dated a few men over the years. I just never got close to any of them."

"That's sad, Maddie."

"Not so sad, actually," Maddie responded with a smile in her voice. "I've had a good life. I bought this little cottage in the 60s, and working at the hospital, I've met lots of people and made many friends."

Sarah remained silent, waiting for Maddie to continue.

"Oh my," Maddie said suddenly. "I've wandered far from the subject. I was talking about the quilt, and how did I ever get this far afield?"

"It's fine, Maddie. I've loved hearing your story."

"Old folks are like that, it seems. If we find someone who'll listen, we talk on and on."

Sarah chuckled and said, "I love listening, so talk all you want."

"Well, I wanted to tell you about the quilt. As much as my mother loved that quilt, I must have ended up loving it even more. It became a symbol of family for me, and it has spent most of its life on my bed. Amazingly, it's stood up this long, although I'm sure you noticed it has blocks that are beginning to disintegrate, and its edges are frayed beyond repair and would have to be completely replaced. I've often thought about repairing the damaged blocks, but then it wouldn't be the same quilt that covered my mother and father all those many years ago."

"It's perfect just the way it is," Sarah remarked. "And Andy loves it too. He also grew up without family. You can't imagine what it means to him to have you in his life now."

"Oh, I certainly do know. Imagine what it's like for me to have this young girl in my home. Did you know that she's the image of Cora Lee?"

Sarah didn't want to point out that Maddie had already told her that. Like so many people that age, Maddie frequently repeated things. Sarah felt it was insensitive to mention it, although she noticed that many people thought nothing of saying, "You already told me that." Instead, she gently changed the subject by asking whether Maddie had any pictures of Cora Lee.

"I don't have any pictures since I didn't take any with me, but I remember her face like it was yesterday. Caitlyn takes after her grandmother. There's no doubt about it."

The two women remained quiet for a few moments, Sarah digesting what she had learned, and Maddie reliving those years in her mind.

Sarah finally said, "I think the poster needs to say that this quilt provided love and comfort to several generations of the family."

"I think that's perfect," Maddie replied with tears in her eyes.

Chapter 9

"Okay," Ruth announced at the next meeting. "I've spoken with the Community Center, and we're scheduled for the first weekend in November." Everyone expressed their excitement and began chattering among themselves. "Settle down," Ruth requested above the noise. "We need to do some serious planning and organizing. That's less than a month away."

"We need to write up everything we know about our quilts so we can post the information next to each quilt," Delores said.

"Sarah has already done that for Andy's quilt," Sophie said. "Show it to them," she added to Sarah.

Sarah pulled out the draft of her sign and passed it around.

"This looks nice, but I can't type," Myrtle said as she examined the sign.

"I think they should all look alike," Anna said. "If everyone wants to write up what you want your sign to say, I'd be happy to do the signs on my computer and print them out on card stock so they'll be uniform."

"Thank you, Anna," several people said in unison.

"What should we include?" Becky asked.

"A description of the quilt, the pattern if you know it, who made it and when …" Ruth began.

Anna finished, saying, "… and any other facts you'd like to include."

"It doesn't have to be typed," Anna added, "but put your name and phone number on the bottom for me in case I have any questions."

"How are we going to hang these quilts?" Becky asked, suddenly realizing that they hadn't discussed the logistics at all.

"I talked to the president of the quilt guild in Hamilton, Betsy Cramer. She's a good friend of mine, and the guild has agreed to loan us their frames for the weekend," Ruth responded. "They don't have a show scheduled this winter."

"How will we get them?" Sophie asked.

"Betsy offered to have them brought to us, and she'll have them picked up after the show. She even offered to have someone help us hang the quilts. I think she's trying to protect the frames," she added with a chuckle, "but I accepted her offer and said that the club would pay for their time. That will make it much easier on us."

"We need to talk about the fee," Sarah said, and Sophie nodded her agreement.

"Since we're offering this at the retirement village," Sophie suggested, "why don't we have it free for residents and charge a small fee to visitors from outside the community, perhaps six dollars. What do you think?"

"I like that," Sarah responded. "But how are these people going to get through the security gate?"

Cunningham Village was a gated community. For the first few years, they had had a guard at the entrance, but with the advances in security technology, the guard had been replaced with a keypad, which allowed residents to tap in their code to open the gate. Visitors could call the resident they were coming to see, who could, in turn, open the gate from their home phone. Sometimes people gave their code out to frequent visitors, but that was discouraged.

"The community representative I spoke with," Ruth responded, "said they'd figure that one out. They might put one of their security people at the gate for the duration of the show and just wave in anyone who says they are there for the event."

"We're just a quiet little community," Sophie whispered to Sarah, "not a munitions arsenal. If you ask me, they make too big a deal out of security."

"Oh, speaking of visitors," Ruth added, "I need to get advertisements out to the community. I'll call the local paper tomorrow."

"Now, let's take a look at the quilts." Ruth had asked everyone to bring in pictures of their quilts so the group could get an idea of what they had for the show.

While the group members were pulling out their photos, Ruth went into the back room and emerged with her arms loaded down. "I brought these from home after my parents died," she said as she spread them out. Ruth had been raised in an Amish community but had left during her late teens.

"I only brought the very old ones. As you can see, these oldest ones were one solid color, but the quilting was very elaborate. See these swirling feathers? They began using more colors later, but only solids like this one with large blocks in bright colors. You'll often find black in Amish quilts as well. I have some with patterns like chains and stars, but I didn't bring those. They are probably not very old."

"How old do you think those solid ones are?" Delores asked.

"They would have been made sometime after 1880. The Amish didn't start quilting until about that time. They were still using featherbeds as coverings until then."

After examining Ruth's quilts, the rest of the group spread out their pictures for everyone to see. Myrtle, one of the older members of the group, reached for her tote bag and pulled out three tattered quilts.

"My grandson takes all the pictures with his phone but he wasn't home, so I just brought my quilts," she said. "I hope that's okay. These belonged to my family long before I was born. I have no idea how old they are, but I know they were old when I was a kid, and I'm into my eighties now." The group was fascinated with the tiny hand stitches as Myrtle unfolded them. Frank appeared to be holding back his comments, but everyone knew he was disturbed by the rips and tears. He shook his head and frowned but remained quiet.

As they went through the pictures, they realized how much they were missing by not being able to see the actual quilts. "I'm so glad we'll have the chance to see all these quilts up close," Christina said as she studied the photos.

"How many do we have?" Sophie asked.

"I was attempting to keep a tally as you presented your quilts," Ruth responded, "and it looks like we'll have about three dozen altogether."

"This will be an incredible show!" Sophie announced.

At that moment, Sarah's cell phone rang. As she had requested, Charles had restored the ringtone of an old-fashioned telephone, and Sarah smiled as she reached into her purse.

Moments later, her expression completely changed. "I'll be right there," she said. Turning to Sophie, she began putting on her coat and said, "I need to leave."

With no other explanation, Sarah hurried out to her car and headed for the local veterinary hospital.

Chapter 10

All Sarah was told when she arrived was that her dog, Barney, had collapsed. She now stood by the examining table with her husband's arm around her as the doctor began to explain the dog's condition and the procedure he was recommending.

Barney, heavily medicated, lay motionless on the table.

"Will he live?" Sarah asked the doctor in a trembling voice.

"As I told your husband, this procedure is your dog's only hope for a normal life. His heart rate is dangerously high, and without the pacemaker, his arrhythmia will, at the very least, impede his ability to live a normal life. In the worst case, it could cause his heart to stop. I recommend we insert a pacemaker immediately, but this is an expensive surgery and something the two of you must decide together. I'll leave you alone so ..."

"That's not necessary, doctor," Sarah responded before the doctor could finish. "I'm completely committed to this dog and have been since the day he and I met at the pound. We want the surgery, right?" Sarah said, turning her eyes toward her husband pleadingly.

"We definitely do," Charles responded as he pulled his now weeping wife into his arms. "Do whatever you need to do, doctor. Just get our dog back on his feet."

"I'd like to ask you a few questions," the doctor began. "I've already done extensive testing and haven't found tumors or any other obvious cause for the arrhythmia. Has he been listless lately?"

"Yes, he has," Sarah responded. "I just attributed it to old age, but we really don't know how old he is."

"Oh, this dog isn't very old. I'd say he's no more than seven or eight. He has a lot of good years ahead of him. I'd like to get him into surgery right away if that's agreeable with you folks, but I want to do some follow-up after the surgery and see if we can find the underlying cause. Who is your current veterinarian?"

"Doctor Baker saw Barney until he retired, and we haven't had a need to take him in since then. At least we didn't realize we did," Sarah added regretfully.

"Then, with your permission, I'll do a few tests tonight while he's under the anesthesia. That will be easier on him."

"Yes, do whatever you need to do," Sarah responded. "May I be alone with him for a few minutes?"

"Of course," the doctor replied with an understanding smile. "I'll leave you folks alone."

He stepped out of the room, and Charles slipped out behind him, saying, "I'll be right out here, honey."

"You don't need to leave," Sarah said, but without much conviction. Charles knew she needed to be alone with her dog. He threw her a kiss and quietly closed the door.

Sarah moved closer to her dog's side and laid her hands on him gently and lovingly. He slowly opened his eyes and looked into hers. "You're going to be okay, boy. You'll be home in no time," she said, trying not to show her concern, but she knew he could read her every emotion. She knew he wanted to comfort her, but he was the one who needed comforting this time. She laid her head on his side and gently stroked him. He closed his eyes and fell back to sleep.

The doctor convinced them to go home, and he promised that he'd call the moment surgery was over. "He'll sleep the rest of the night, so you folks can come back in the morning and see him."

* * * * *

"We have time for breakfast, Sarah," Charles told his wife in response to her desire to leave for the animal hospital immediately. "The doctor won't even be there. He said to come after they open and he's had a chance to check him out."

"You mean they left him alone all night?" she responded frantically.

"No, Sarah. That young assistant you met was there all night, and the doctor lives a block away. He said for us to come around 10:00 this morning."

"But," Sarah began, and then realized she was letting her fears control her. The doctor had called just before midnight and said the surgery had been a success, and Barney was sleeping comfortably.

Sarah sighed and finally agreed. "Okay, we'll go at 10:00. Let's have oatmeal with raisins." Charles smiled, knowing that his wife always turned to oatmeal with raisins when she needed comfort food in the morning.

"Did the doctor tell you much about the actual surgery?" Sarah asked.

"Yes, he said that he made a small incision in Barney's neck for the pacemaker and the leads, which he would be feeding through a vein to his heart." He saw his wife quickly wipe away a tear as she served the oatmeal.

"How long do you think they'll keep him?" she asked.

"A few days, I guess. I'm sure he'll be home just as soon as the doctor thinks it's safe."

But as it turned out, they were able to pick up Barney later that day, after promising to keep him at home and quiet. The doctor felt he would remain calmer at home. "He'll need a month of rest," the doctor told them as they were preparing to leave. Once they got all their instructions and Barney's medications, Charles carefully carried him to the car, wrapped in a small quilt.

He rode home on Sarah's lap and slept. When they arrived home, Charles carried him into the house and laid him in his bed, which now had freshly washed blankets and Charles' travel pillow.

Now this is the life, Barney must have been thinking, as he noticed that his water bowl, which was now within easy reach of his bed, was filled with chicken broth.

Chapter 11

"How's Barney?" Caitlyn asked. Caitlyn had called Sarah every day since she learned about Barney's surgery.

"He's doing fine," Sarah responded with a happy lilt in her voice. "It's getting a little hard to keep him down. He keeps getting up and carrying his ball to Charles, then me, trying to get someone to play with him. Charles has been sitting on the floor by Barney's bed for the past hour playing 'leave it / take it' with tiny treats just to entertain him."

"Did Papa tell you he's decided to come here for Christmas?" Caitlyn asked.

"Yes, and I'm so glad you will all be together for the holidays."

"I'm glad too," Caitlyn responded. "Aunt Maddie is dying to meet him."

"And maybe you're a little excited about it, too?"

"Oh, Aunt Sarah! You know I am. I was hoping he'd come, but, of course, that means I'm not coming there and won't be able to see you and Uncle Charles and everyone else. But that's actually why I'm calling. Would you two like to come here for Christmas? Aunt Maddie said if you were planning to drive, you could bring Barney too, but it's an eight- or nine-hour trip so you might want to fly. What do you think?"

"Sweetie, I'll talk to Charles about it, but I think this should be a private family time for you, your dad, and your aunt. It's a perfect chance for you three to bond as a family."

"You're family, too, Aunt Sarah," Caitlyn replied, but her tone suggested that she understood.

They talked for a while about school and the upcoming quilt show and said goodbye just as Charles was walking into the kitchen.

"Was that Caitlyn?" he asked.

"Yes." She told him about the invitation and what she had told Caitlyn. "I completely agree," he responded. "Let's leave them alone to enjoy Christmas together. Besides, we have our grandchildren to be with."

"You're right, Charles. I want to be here with the kids. Caitlyn understands."

"Besides," Charles added, "I was hoping you and I could have a little vacation after Christmas. We could get away from the cold weather and head down south somewhere."

"Such as?" Sarah asked with a glint in her eye. "Another cruise, perhaps?" she added playfully. "The one we took was pretty romantic, as I remember."

"Well, it sure was," Charles responded rather matter-of-factly. "I was busy courting you, as I recall."

"Oh, you were, were you?"

"You were a difficult one, too," he added. "You were determined not to get serious with me. What happened, I wonder," he teased.

"I decided you weren't a bad catch, so I let you win me over."

"Oh, so it was all your doing," he responded, continuing the flirtatious banter.

At that moment, the phone rang, and Sarah walked over to answer it, tossing a coy look over her shoulder.

"Sophie! No, you aren't interrupting anything," she said, winking at her husband and walking toward her sewing room with her phone. "What's up?"

"I've been thinking about this quilt show and realizing this is going to be lots of work. I hope I didn't start something that is going to be too much for us. We don't have many people in the club, and …"

"Sophie, we'll be fine," Sarah assured her friend. "Once the quilts are on display, we'll sit back and enjoy watching the community marvel over them. It sounds like we'll have quite a crowd. I was talking with Margory last week …"

"Margory? Do I know her?"

"Sure you do. She's the head of the Resource Room at the Community Center. She said that lots of people have called about it. Since it's at the Center, people assume she knows all about it, so she called me to get the details. I referred her to Ruth, but it sounds like there'll be a crowd just from our community."

"What got me concerned," Sophie responded, "was the announcement in the newspaper. Ruth has a spread about it and encouraged people to come, and at six dollars a person, it's cheap entertainment. I think we'll have a lot of people from town. What are we going to do with them all?"

"Sophie, we aren't going to do anything except take their money and point them toward the quilts. As a matter of fact,

I was going to ask you if you'd like to be one of the folks at the front door. You'd be sitting down, and you can switch off with a few other people. You could have short shifts."

"I'd like that, and I'd get to see everyone," Sophie responded eagerly. "What are you going to do?"

"I thought I'd manage our white-glove crew. Quilters know all about white-glove ladies, but there will be non-quilters there who will have to be taught not to touch the quilts, and if they want to see the back, a lady in white gloves can carefully lift it for them."

"Should we make *Do not touch* signs?"

"Ruth has some already, which we'll post, but she told me that the signs tend to make people want to touch."

"So you don't think I've created a monster?" Sophie asked, still sounding worried.

"I think you created a great activity for our club. In fact, I've been thinking about making up a flyer about our Tuesday Night Quilters."

"That's a great idea, Sarah. I'll hand them out and talk about the group to any quilters who come."

"And point them to Ruth's stand. She'll be selling fabric and patterns, and she's doing up a flyer about her classes. We just might recruit a few new quilters as well!"

"If I have created a monster," Sophie responded thoughtfully, "perhaps it will turn out to be a good monster."

Chapter 12

The day finally came. Sarah and Sophie arrived at the Community Center at 8:00, and the custodian was waiting for them as planned. He let them into the auditorium, which had been enlarged to include the multipurpose room next door.

Sophie gasped when she stepped into the room. "This is outstanding! I had no idea. . . ." She rested her right hand on her heart as her eyes traveled across the room, taking in the rows of quilts neatly hanging from wooden frames. "This looks just like a real quilt show," she added.

"It *is* a real quilt show," Sarah responded with a chuckle as she put her arm around her friend's shoulder. "And you did it!"

"I had no idea. . . ." Sophie repeated, still mesmerized by the view.

Pulling her friend out of her trance, Sarah said, "Okay, here is your place over here." She led Sophie to a six-foot table already arranged with five chairs, pads of paper, a cup of pens, and several stacks of handouts that Ruth and her sister Anna had prepared in advance.

"Why so many chairs? I thought this was just my job."

"Some of our club members will want to sit with you, and you might need help at some point. If the visitors come in droves, you'll need help collecting their money and making change."

"Oh, I forgot about change," Sophie exclaimed anxiously.

"No problem," Ruth responded, walking in the door at that moment. "I brought a few things from the shop, and here's my cashbox loaded with small bills." She placed the box on the table in front of Sophie, who was now sitting. "And here's my hand calculator. You might not need this, but I can't make change without it. I haven't been able to subtract accurately since grade school."

"We're all technology dependent these days," Andy announced as he sauntered into the hall. He immediately turned his attention to the arrangement of the frames and said, "The boys did a nice job." He and Charles had met the Hamilton crew the evening before and supervised the installation of the frames. Ruth and Sarah, along with a few of the club members, joined them later in the evening to oversee the hanging of the quilts. "Looks pretty good," Andy added as he examined the first few frames in each row.

Nathan, Ruth's husband, entered pushing a large cart loaded with boxes and bolts of fabric. "Did they get your booth set up?" he asked his wife as he headed toward the area they had saved for her shop display.

"I didn't realize you were selling fabric by the yard," Sarah commented. "Will you need help?"

"Anna will be here before we open, and Nathan is great at cutting fabric. As for the bolts, I realized that we'll have quilters here who will get inspired by the show and might want to buy fabric and patterns right away."

"That was a great idea, Ruth," Sarah responded, following the Weavers back to their vendor booth.

"I mostly brought reproduction fabrics from the 1800s and early 1900s, along with a large assortment of pre-cuts. Sophie," she suddenly called out, "be sure to give everyone my flyer and tell them about the 20% coupon. It's only good this weekend."

"Will do," Sophie responded as she got organized at the welcome table. She had brought handwork but realized she probably wouldn't have time to work on it. She remembered watching quilters at previous quilt shows working on their projects. "We should have had a raffle quilt," she abruptly announced, remembering that most of the quilters she had seen at shows had been sitting by raffle quilts and sewing between customers. "Why didn't we think of that?"

"Next time," Sarah called out from one of the aisles.

"Where are you?"

"Over here, looking at Mabel's quilts. She sent two we didn't see before. I think they are probably the oldest ones here. She said this one was made by her great-great-grandmother."

"Isn't Mabel in her eighties?" Sophie hollered, wishing her friend would move closer. Sophie hadn't admitted to anyone that she had been fitted for a hearing aid the previous week and was still learning how to use it. "That one must be at least 150 years old!"

"At least," Sarah responded.

"A feast?" Sophie asked excitedly. "When?"

"What are you asking about?" Charles inquired as he sat down by Sophie.

"Oh, I didn't know you were here."

"I just got here," he responded. "Sarah sent me home to pick up some things she intended to bring."

"For the feast?" Sophie asked eagerly.

"What feast?" Sarah asked as she approached the welcome table and gave her husband a brief hug. "What's this about a feast?"

"These darn hearing aids need an adjustment," Sophie muttered under her breath.

Two hours later, people began to arrive, and by 11:00 the parking lot was filled and a tour bus had just pulled up in front of the Center.

"We should have arranged for a food vendor," Sophie announced to anyone who would listen.

"I'm sending people over to the café," Sarah responded as she walked by the welcome table, "but they can only accommodate a few at a time. Tell people where the local restaurants are," she added. *We should have made a restaurant handout as well*, Sarah realized. *There's more to throwing a quilt show than we thought.*

At the end of the day, as the last of the visitors were leaving, the group let out a collective sigh. "Well, that's day one. Can we take another day like this?" Sarah asked rhetorically.

"Tomorrow won't be this busy since we're only open from 1:00 to 5:00."

"That's not necessarily true," Sophie responded. "We might have just as many people but scrunched into less time."

As Ruth walked up, Charles stood to give her his chair. "Such a gentleman you married," she said to Sarah as she sat down with a deep exhalation. "What a day!"

"Sales were good, I take it," Sarah commented.

"Phenomenal!" Ruth replied. "I'll need to bring more bolts tomorrow. I sold most of the Civil War collection in the first few hours. Our customers loved the old quilts. You know, most quilt shows these days feature modern designs and bright, flashy fabrics, but I think the old-fashioned quilts still touch our souls like no others can."

"I agree," Sophie responded. "They bring up buried memories for me. I don't remember the specific quilts from my childhood, but I can feel the emotions as I look at these quilts. They take me back in time."

"To a simpler time?" Andy asked.

"Yes, to a simpler time," Sophie agreed.

"I don't know if it was actually any simpler," Charles speculated. "Every generation of old folks talks about the 'good old days,' and I'll admit that it sure seems simpler in retrospect, but if we were back there now, struggling financially and living without modern conveniences, we probably wouldn't say it was simple."

The exhausted group sat quietly for a few minutes, contemplating what had been said when Charles suddenly announced, "Time for pizza. Let's go, gang."

* * * * *

Sarah and Charles got up late the next morning and prepared a pancake and bacon breakfast to build up their strength for another day of being on their feet. "I'm going to suggest that the club develop a list of things to do ahead of time in preparation for a quilt show."

"You're going to do this again?" Charles asked doubtfully.

"Not necessarily, but while the show is fresh on our minds, it would be a good chance to brainstorm and get it all down on paper, particularly the things we didn't do but should have."

"Good idea, but I hope that next show doesn't come along any time soon."

"Oh, it won't," Sarah responded as she put her hands on her lower back and stretched. "That was too much standing for all of us. And adding available resting places will be on the top of my list."

"How late do you think we'll be staying tonight?" Charles asked.

"The Hamilton crew will be coming immediately after we close the doors," Sarah responded. "Ruth said it will probably take them an hour to get all the quilts down and another hour to dismantle the frames."

"What time are the quilters coming to pick up their quilts?"

"Ruth and her husband had a splendid idea. They are taking the quilts home with them in their van. That will save lots of time this evening, and we won't have the distraction of quilt owners coming and going. More coffee?"

As Sarah was pouring their coffee, the phone rang. "Andy, good morning. I hope you are rested and ready for another day of …" She stopped talking abruptly and looked aghast.

"What's going on?" Charles asked when he saw the look on his wife's face.

Sarah hit the speaker button. "… gone," Andy was saying.

"Your quilt is gone?" Charles called out from across the room.

"My quilt. All the quilts! They're gone," Andy responded in a shattered voice. "Every last quilt is gone."

Chapter 13

Charles hurried across the kitchen, and Sarah handed him the phone. "What's going on, Andy? It sounded like you said the quilts are gone. What are you talking about?"

"I got here early to help Ruth restock her booth, and when we stepped into the auditorium, it was empty. Completely empty! Well, the frames are still here, but some of them are broken, and the quilts are gone. It looks like someone just yanked them off the frames and took off."

"How can that be?" Charles responded as he looked at his wife. Her palms were pressed against her cheeks, and her eyes were wide open in shock. She looked pale. He reached over and gently pulled her to his side and wrapped his arm around her.

"What are we going to do, Charles?" Andy asked, sounding desperate. "I should have been here. I said I'd provide security, and I didn't even stay, but I figured it was locked up …" Andy was blubbering at this point. "… and what are we going to tell these women, and, oh my, I just remembered Aunt Maddie. What will I tell her? I promised to take care of her quilt.…"

"Andy," Charles said sharply. "Breathe. I'm on my way over. Just sit tight. We'll get to the bottom of this. He couldn't have gotten far with them. He may have stashed them somewhere and was planning to come back for them. Have you notified Security?"

"You know we don't have a security force anymore," Andy replied with obvious anger.

"Right," Charles responded, muttering a few unintelligible words. "The cost-saving initiative! Well, how about the custodian?"

"Lonnie Dunkin is here. He's the maintenance supervisor, but he doesn't work nights."

"I know Lonnie," Charles responded.

Charles knew Lonnie Dunkin well. Charles had met him when Lonnie's brother, Larry, was being tried and ultimately incarcerated for the murder of the foreman who built Charles and Sarah's current home. Lonnie's brother had sat by silently as Charles himself was arrested for the crime. Charles never blamed Larry for the death, believing that he was basically a good man and had only been acting in self-defense. Charles was instrumental in getting Lonnie the job as the maintenance supervisor for the Community Center and nursing home in Cunningham Village, and they developed a lasting friendship.

"Tell Lonnie I want to speak with him. Has anyone called the police?"

"I called over to the administrator's office. Holbrooke said he'd take care of that. He's on his way here now."

"Holbrooke," Charles repeated. "That name sounds familiar."

"Jeff Holbrooke. You know him from the case this past summer," Sarah whispered. "He's the administrator of the nursing home and the Community Center."

"Right," Charles said, returning his attention to Andy on the phone. "I'm on my way, buddy. Just sit tight."

"I'm going with you," Sarah announced emphatically as Charles was hanging up.

"Of course," he responded, kissing her forehead.

As they were heading toward the car, Sarah stopped suddenly. "I should call Sophie."

"We'll call her from the Center. I want to see this for myself before we start telling people about it. There might be an easy explanation."

"You don't really believe that, do you?"

"No," her husband admitted despondently. "I'm afraid not."

* * * * *

Two police cars were pulling up as Sarah and Charles arrived. Detective Halifax looked at the approaching couple as he stepped out of the car. "I figured you'd be mixed up in this somehow," he said gruffly but extended his hand to greet Charles. The two had a history together, primarily through their old lieutenant, Matt Stokely, who had died the previous year.

"Hal," Charles said as they shook hands. "You know my wife, Sarah."

"Sure do," the detective said with a frown. "Where's your sidekick today?" The detective was accustomed to seeing Sarah and Sophie together, usually at the police station being reprimanded for interfering in police business.

Sarah simply smiled and said, "It's good to see you, Detective Halifax. I'm sure you'll get to the bottom of this."

Halifax grunted and turned to a young cop standing nearby. "Is Holbrooke here yet?"

"He's over there."

"Excuse me, folks. I have work to do," Halifax grumbled. He started to walk away, but stopped and turned toward the couple. "Stay put. I want to talk to you both."

"Is that his polite way of saying, 'Don't leave town'?" Sarah whispered. "Does he think we had something to do with this?"

"Of course not, hon. That's just his way. Let's see if they'll let us go inside. I want to get a look at the crime scene."

"Crime scene?" Sarah exclaimed. "Our nice quilt show has become a 'crime scene'?"

"It's just police talk. A crime happened here, so it's a crime scene. It doesn't mean anything beyond that."

"Well, I don't like it," Sarah declared adamantly.

"What's going on?" The voice was shrill and coming at them at a frightening speed.

"Sophie! Slow that thing down before you kill yourself or somebody else. What are you doing on a mobility scooter anyway?"

"Norman bought it for me. Isn't it great? Now I can go all over the community without my car. Do you want to take a ride?"

Before Sarah could find the words to respond to her outrageous friend, Sophie noticed the police cars. "Hey," she said. "What's going on?"

"You take your friend aside," Charles said, "and catch her up while I see if I can get past the yellow tape. Maybe Hal can get me in."

"What's going on?" Sophie repeated, beginning to realize it was something big.

"Drive over here by the benches where we can talk," Sarah responded as she led the way, hoping not to get run over. Once they were settled, Sarah told Sophie what little she knew, and, as expected, her friend was horrified.

"Our quilts? *All* our quilts? This can't be. I have to get home and get my card file. We have work to do!" As a self-proclaimed amateur sleuth, Sophie had developed a card file method for recording clues, which she believed had been instrumental in solving several crimes in the community.

"Calm down, Sophie, and stay right here. We're waiting to see what happened. Charles is inside now, and I saw Detective Halifax go in right after him. Charles will get the facts. All I know is what Andy told me this morning. All the quilts were missing from the auditorium when he went in."

Sometime later, Sarah saw Charles and Detective Halifax, followed by Jeffery Holbrooke, heading toward them. The detective looked angry. "What do you mean you had no control over who came in?" he was saying, obviously to the administrator. "This is a gated community. How did all those people get through the gate without signing in?"

"We don't sign people in anymore. We have a keypad, and you just punch in your code, or, if you're a visitor, you call in, and the resident can buzz you in."

"That's not what I asked. How did the visitors to the quilt show get in?"

"Well, at first they called into the Community Center, and we buzzed them in, but …"

"Yes?" the detective was attempting to remain calm but looked exasperated.

"Well, there were just too many, and it was continuous, so we opened the gate."

"And just let everyone in?" the detective asked.

"Yes, but …"

"So much for security," the detective grumbled. "Did you folks know about this?" he asked, turning to Charles and Sarah.

"Security isn't our responsibility," Andy said in an angry voice as he joined the group. "That's management's job," he added, giving Holbrooke an intense look. Andy had played a key role in the fight against management's desire to save money by eliminating the security guard at the front gate. His side lost, and guards were replaced by keypads the previous year.

"We need to get on with the investigation. Who's in charge of this quilt show?"

No one answered, but everyone looked at one another.

"Ruth, I guess," Sarah responded. "Actually, it's our whole quilt club, Hal. We put this on together, and I don't know who I would say is in charge. No one, really. We did this as a group."

"Who's this Ruth you mentioned?"

"She's the owner of Running Stitches, the quilt shop where our club meets. She had a vendor's booth here. Oh!" Sarah said abruptly. "Charles, did he take anything from her booth?"

"No, Ruth said her booth was untouched. They must have only been interested in the quilts."

"I need to talk with everyone involved with this quilt show," Detective Halifax said, turning to Charles. "Could you get me a list of names and phone numbers? We'll meet at the station this afternoon."

"Hal, let me make a suggestion," Charles said, noting that his friend was looking tired and sounding impatient. "Sarah and I will pull everyone together at our house this afternoon, and you can come by and question them all at one time. How would that be?"

"Unorthodox, to say the least, but an improvement over anything I can think of. Tell them to bring a description of everything they had in the show, so we'll know what we're looking for."

"We can do you one better than that," Sarah responded. "Ruth has pictures of all the quilts."

"Well, be sure she comes this afternoon and have her bring all the photos."

"We'll see you at the house around 3:00," Charles said as he suddenly caught sight of Sophie sitting on a bright red three-wheel mobility scooter. "What the ..."

"Norman got it for me. Isn't it great? Hop on, and I'll take you for a ride."

"I think I'll skip that for now. Hal wants to question everyone at our house this afternoon at 3:00."

"I'll be there. Does anyone need a ride?" Sophie asked, looking at Andy and Jeff Holbrooke, who both turned away quickly.

As Sarah and Charles were walking home, Sophie sped past them on her new red scooter. "See you at 3:00," she hollered and waved, temporarily losing control of the scooter, which wobbled precariously.

"That's a disaster waiting to happen," Charles commented as he watched his wife's best friend swerving to avoid a parked car.

"One disaster at a time," Sarah responded.

Chapter 14

Sarah and Ruth divided the membership list and were able to track down everyone except Mabel, who was out of town visiting her grandchildren. In addition to the club members, Jeff Holbrooke was coming and said he'd bring Lonnie, the maintenance supervisor.

Jeff and Lonnie arrived first, and Charles took the opportunity to ask Lonnie about his cleaning staff. "I contract for them with this cleaning outfit out of Chicago. They have clients all over the state."

"Do you have regular people?"

"Yeah, they're just regular guys. . . ." Lonnie said, looking confused by the question.

"No, I meant, do you have the same people every day?"

"Oh, I gotcha. Yeah, we usually have the same gals, but the men aren't always the same."

"Do you check them out?"

"Nah. Their company does all that."

Charles made a mental note to tell Hal that the cleaning company would be a good place to start. He'd like to see the background checks himself if Hal would allow it. In fact, he hoped to help out with the investigation. When Matt was alive, he would occasionally hire Charles for a special assignment.

By the time Detective Halifax arrived, most of the club members were there. Ruth had met them individually at the door to explain what had happened. Most of the members took the news in stride, although Sarah caught several surreptitiously wiping away tears. *Lost memories,* Sarah thought, wondering if there was any chance of recovering the missing quilts.

While Charles introduced the detective to the quilters he knew, Sarah picked Barney up in her arms and carried him to their bedroom, where he had a bed and several of his quilts. "Now, you stay here and take a nap. You're still on bed rest, you know," she said in a soft, loving tone. Barney sighed and closed his eyes as Sarah gently closed the door.

After everyone was seated in the Parkers' living room, the detective explained what had happened and what the department would be doing. He said he wanted to speak with everyone before they left. "You may know something that could develop into an important lead. Just tell the investigator anything that comes to your mind that you might have seen or heard during the day."

Hal had brought four investigators with him who would be questioning the club members. He intended to speak with Andy, Charles, Holbrooke, and the maintenance supervisor himself. He would also question anyone the investigators identified as needing a second look.

They spread out all over the Parkers' house, and the time went quickly. Suddenly Sarah noticed that the sun had set and it was after 6:00 in the evening. "These are my friends, Hal. I want to offer them something to eat."

"But this isn't a party, Sarah. We need to keep going. The guys have gotten some good information. I just want to get your quilts back. I'm not the enemy."

"I know, Hal. I'll wait another half hour, and then I'm ordering pizza if you aren't ready to let these folks go home."

"I'll be finished by then."

Exhausted from a very long and intense day, Sarah, Charles, Sophie, and Andy sat in the living room with their feet up. Everyone had left a little after 6:30, as Hal had promised. The pizza had arrived, and Charles had ordered sodas as well since he wasn't sure if he should offer beer. Andy had been a long-standing member of Alcoholics Anonymous, and Charles didn't want to tempt him in light of his current mood. His friend was feeling responsible for the theft since he had assured the club that he'd provide security.

"These gals need beer with their pizza," Andy announced when he saw the sodas arrive. Charles explained privately why he had ordered the sodas, and Andy laughed. "You don't have to worry about me, friend. I learned my lesson and learned it well. In fact, when I realized how guilty I was feeling about all this, I called my sponsor right away. We talked it out. Pass me one of those sodas, fella," and they exchanged an understanding fist bump.

"So, Charles, what did they learn?"

"I have no idea. I couldn't get anything out of Hal. I told him I'd like to be included in the investigation, and he didn't respond, but then on his way out the door he turned to me and said, 'Come by the station tomorrow.' So what does that mean?"

"He either wants your help," Andy began, "or he suspects you of Grand Theft Quilt."

* * * * *

"Oh, Papa, that's terrible! I can't imagine all those quilts being stolen at once. How did they do it? Was there a whole gang?" Caitlyn asked.

"We don't have any idea, honey. I'm just feeling so bad about Aunt Maddie's quilt. We might get them all back, but in the meantime …"

"Papa, I know you don't like keeping secrets, but I think it's best if we don't tell her yet. Why worry her, when there's always the chance that the police will find them. And you said Uncle Charles might be working on it, too, right?"

"Yes, he is, and it just happened last night. I shouldn't be discouraged yet," Andy responded. "Okay, for now let's not worry Aunt Maddie. It's going to be hard to be there at Christmas without mentioning it. I know she'll ask about the quilt, and I really don't want to lie to her."

"You also don't want to ruin her Christmas, Papa. She's so excited about meeting you and the three of us celebrating Christmas together. She's already asked me to take her shopping, and she wants to know what kinds of things you like."

"Oh, gifts! I hadn't thought about that. I don't know what to get her either."

"Then I'll be taking you shopping too. Come a few days early, and we'll shop. And I have a couple of places I want to take you. This will be such fun!"

"I'm convinced. I don't want to ruin Christmas. What are you two doing for Thanksgiving?"

"Aunt Maddie has invited a few of her close friends. Everyone is bringing a dish, and I'm cooking the turkey. I don't have any idea how, but I didn't tell Aunt Maddie that. I'm going to call Aunt Sarah."

Andy loved hearing all the references to aunts and uncles, even though most of them weren't actually relatives. It just sounded great for his daughter to be enjoying the warmth of family.

"And what are you doing on Thanksgiving?" Caitlyn asked.

"I'm not sure," Andy responded. "Sarah and Charles invited me to come to their house. They're having family, though, and I hate to intrude."

"Who's coming?"

"Well, there's Sarah's son, Jason, and his wife, Jennifer, and their two little ones, and Sarah's daughter, Martha, along with Martha's husband, Timothy."

"And his daughter, Penny?" Caitlyn asked.

"Yes, Penny will be coming too."

"Which I guess would mean Sophie will be there, since she's Sarah's best friend and Timothy's mom?" Caitlyn asked.

"Of course."

"Well, I think it makes perfect sense for you to be there. That makes a complete package of friends who have become family."

"I guess you're right," Andy responded thoughtfully. "We're one carefully crafted family, aren't we?"

"We sure are! Goodnight, Papa."

Chapter 15

"Well, that was disappointing."

Charles had just returned from the police station, where he had been briefed on the case. Unfortunately, he didn't have any good news to report.

"They don't have a single lead," Charles told his wife. "The chief is meeting with the press this afternoon and will encourage members of the public to call in if they saw anything, but he's not optimistic. The newspaper article didn't stir up any calls."

"And no fingerprints at the scene?"

"Oh, yes, hundreds of fingerprints—everyone who has touched the doorknobs, the quilt frames, and the sink faucets this weekend. They are hoping for leads that might come from the public, but Hal said those calls don't usually pan out. He has cops knocking on doors in the Village looking for someone who might have seen something Saturday night. This happened sometime between closing and when Andy went in around 8:00 Sunday morning, most likely in the dead of night."

"While our community of old folks was sleeping," Sarah remarked as she freshened her husband's coffee and reached into his jar of fat-free cookies. She noticed a look of despair cross his face and, instead, put the lid back on the jar of fat-free cookies and reached into the cupboard for a box of gourmet cookies that she had on hand primarily for guests. With a history of strokes, Charles was on an extremely restrictive diet, which Sarah made sure he adhered to most of the time. Occasionally it seemed more important to set the diet aside and experience the pleasure of eating something special.

"Really?" Charles remarked with a raised eyebrow as Sarah placed the small plate in front of him. "What's the occasion?"

"I love you," she responded as she poured herself another cup of coffee.

"Well, if this is what you feed me when you love me, you must not think much of me the rest of the time."

"Now Charles, you know ..."

"Just kidding, sweetie. I know why you keep me on the heart diet, and I love you for it." The couple had only been married a few years, both having lost their previous partners after many years of marriage. They both knew the pain of loss and would do anything to prolong their time together.

"So, what's next?" Sarah asked. "Did Hal agree to let you work on the case?"

"He did. He said it would have to be unofficial, and I can't charge the department, but I wouldn't want to anyway. I just want to be a part of the investigation. I have a few ideas."

"So do I," Sarah announced enthusiastically.

"Oh?" he responded cautiously. His wife and her best friend had a history of thrusting themselves into police investigations and receiving strong reprimands as a result.

"Don't worry," she said, reassuring him. "I was reading an article in one of my old quilt magazines this morning about locating lost quilts. I'm going to write an article about the theft and include as many pictures as they will accept. Maybe someone will see one of the quilts somewhere. Why would someone steal them unless they planned to sell them? We don't know where they might show up, and these magazines go to quilters all over the country."

"That's a good idea, but I'd like to run it past Hal first. I don't want to do anything that might jeopardize the investigation."

"I don't see how it could, but I'll go ahead and write the article. I'll get Ruth to help with that, and you let me know what he says."

"Deal," Charles responded as he slowly chewed the last cookie with closed eyes, savoring the treat his taste buds had almost forgotten.

* * * * *

"Did you see the police chief on television?" Sophie asked excitedly. "He did a great job. I'll bet we get our quilts back!"

Sarah wasn't feeling as optimistic about their chances, but she had to admit he had done a good job.

"Charles said they already got one call," Sarah said as she carried the phone to a nearby chair. "But it was from someone offering to contribute a couple of old quilts to the people who lost them. A very kind gesture, but another quilt doesn't replace the lost memories. I'll call and thank her anyway."

Sarah told her friend about the article she was writing for the quilt magazines. "Ruth suggested we put it online as well. Her own website reaches thousands of people, and she said she would ask other quilt shops to do the same."

"Great idea," Sophie responded. "Are you ready for a spin on my new scooter?"

"Sophie, I didn't see any place for a second person. Am I going to be sitting on your lap?"

"No, silly. You can drive it yourself. I'll bring it up, and you run it up and down Sycamore Court. Charles and I will sit out front and watch."

"I'll give it a try," Sarah responded, eager to please her friend, who was so excited about her new toy.

"I have another call, Sophie. Come on over." She hung up and answered the second call. "Hello?"

Chapter 16

The caller introduced herself as Myra Prichard. "I live here in the Village, and I heard the police chief this morning talking about the theft. I have something I wanted to tell someone, but I'm embarrassed to call in to the station about this. It seems like such a silly thing, but it just might be important. I don't know what to do. Could I tell you about it instead?"

"You certainly can tell me, Myra, but you might also need to tell the police, depending on what it is. Do you mind if I put you on speaker? I'd like for my husband to hear."

"Oh my, I'd be embarrassed. It's such a silly thing. . . ."

"It's okay, Myra. My husband is a very kind and understanding man. I hope you'll let him hear about it too."

"Well, okay," she said reluctantly.

Sarah motioned for Charles to come closer to the phone, and she handed him the message pad and a pen. He smiled and nodded.

"Go ahead, Myra," Sarah said.

"Okay, but I told you it's silly. I was at the quilt show, and there was this woman back by the ladies' room. She was sort of stooped over—you know, like some old folks get—and she was dressed pretty weird."

"Weird?"

"Well, first of all, she was dressed strangely. None of her clothes went together, and nothing fit. I think her dress might have even been on backward, but I'm not sure. Everything just hung on her. She just looked odd is all," the caller added. "Oh, and she wore a hat with a veil down over part of her face. How long has it been since anyone wore a hat with a veil? It just seemed odd."

"Okay, I agree it seems odd, but …"

"I'm not finished. You see, just as they announced that the show was closing in five minutes, she went into the bathroom. Not the main ladies' room, but that small individual one. I thought that was odd, too."

"Maybe she didn't have time to go back to the main ladies' room," Sarah suggested. *This sounds like a crank call, and I'll bet we'll be getting them for months*, she told herself.

"Well, I had to get up to the front door before I got closed in myself, and I walk very slow. I had a knee replacement last year and never got full use of it back. I did all the exercises like I was told, but that knee was never as good as Maggie's knee. Do you know Maggie? Maggie Swanson? Well," the woman continued without waiting for Sarah's response, "she had hers done this year, and she walks just fine."

Sarah sighed.

"Anyway, since I had to leave and I didn't want this woman to get stuck in the auditorium, I knocked on the door and told her the show was closing. She didn't answer at first, so I knocked harder."

"Did she finally answer?"

"Yes, finally this squeaky voice said, 'Thank you,' but she still didn't come out. I tried the door, but it was locked. There wasn't anything else I could do, and I had to get across the auditorium, so I just left her there. After I got home, I realized that I should have told someone she was in there."

"Do you think you could describe her?"

"I just did."

"Would you mind speaking to my husband, Myra? He's right here, and he wants to ask you a question."

"Oh my, I didn't want to talk to a man about this. I feel so silly. This is nothing."

"Please, Myra. He's a very nice man, and he just has a quick question. His name is Charlie." Sarah handed the phone to her husband and gave him an apologetic look, knowing how much he disliked the nickname, but she thought it would sound less threatening to Myra.

"Hi, Myra. This is Charlie, and I'm very glad you called. I think this will be very helpful information."

"Really?" Myra asked. "I thought it sounded a little crazy."

"Not at all. I think it could be very valuable to the police. Would you consider going in to talk to a friend of mine at the station?"

"Oh no," Myra responded. "I couldn't do that."

"Please consider it, Myra. I think it would be especially helpful if you could describe this woman to a sketch artist so he could draw a picture of her. Sarah and I would go with you."

"You really think that would help?"

"I really do, Myra. I'm so glad you called. Will you let us take you?"

"Well, I guess I could do it, but this woman was old and frail-looking. I don't think she could steal all those quilts."

"That's very true, Myra, but she might know something, or she might have seen something important. Let's see if we can help the police find her, okay?"

"Okay," Myra responded reluctantly. Charles handed the phone back to Sarah with a smile, and she got Myra's address and agreed to pick her up in fifteen minutes.

"I figured we'd better get Myra into our car before she changes her mind," Sarah said as she hung up. "By the way, what are you hoping to learn? I agree with Myra that a frail elderly woman would have a hard time getting one quilt off its frame, much less escaping with them all."

"One elderly woman? That's true. But who says she was really an elderly woman? Who says she was a woman at all?"

* * * * *

"Where are you?" Sophie demanded when Sarah picked up her cell phone.

"Oh, Sophie, I forgot to call you. I'm so sorry." She went on to explain about the call from Myra and what they were doing at the police station.

"Well, I've been sitting out here in front of your house with my scooter running, but you have a good excuse. I'll forgive you, but only if you two will go out with Norman and me tonight. We're going to that Mexican restaurant over on Nicholson Lane."

"The new one? We'd love to. I'll call you when we get home. Who knows, we might even have good news by then."

But after observing Myra and the sketch artist for only a few minutes, it became clear that they weren't going to have any good news to report to Sophie. Myra could describe the woman's numerous outfits in minute detail, but height, weight, facial features, identifying marks—none of these details were stored in Myra's rather sketchy memory. "Don't forget the hat," she kept saying even though the artist told her he would like to fill in some of the woman's facial features rather than cover them with a veil.

"Well, that was wasted time," Sarah announced after she and Charles took Myra to her door.

"Not necessarily," Charles remarked.

"What do you mean? All we know is what she was wearing. How does that help?"

"We'll see. Hal seemed interested. He wouldn't tell me why, but he was smiling when he joined us after looking at the sketches. I had the feeling he knows something he's not ready to share."

"I can't imagine what, but if so, I hope it leads to the quilts. Ruth said she's talked to the quilters and they are devastated by the loss, despite the brave faces they wore Sunday afternoon at our house."

"I'm sure they are," Charles remarked, becoming more serious. "We'll find those quilts. I have a feeling the answer is right under our nose."

Sarah giggled. "Remember the time Andy's missing quilt turned up right under our nose? My nose, at least."

"Barney had dragged it under your bed!" Charles chuckled as he reflected on those early days of their courtship. He was never sure he would win this lovely lady's hand.

He reached over and gently took her hand in his.

Chapter 17

Sarah had just arrived at Running Stitches, where she was going to be teaching a beginning quilt class to a group of homeschooled youngsters. Ruth met her at the door looking worried.

"Sarah, don't you think we should cancel the quilt club meeting tomorrow night?" Ruth was concerned about how upset the group was about the loss of the quilts and the lack of progress the police were making. "No one will want to sew," she added.

"That's true, Ruth. Everyone is experiencing a wide range of emotions, but it might be good to offer a place where our friends can talk about it. Almost everyone in the club has suffered a significant loss this week, and who could be more understanding than their fellow quilters?"

"You're right. We need each other right now."

"Not everyone will want to talk about their feelings, and some people even prefer to be alone at times like this, but I think we should offer the meeting, so everyone has the opportunity if they want."

"You're a smart lady, my friend," Ruth said as she put an arm around Sarah's shoulder and led her into the classroom.

"I'm excited about this class," Sarah said as she began setting up the classroom. "I love seeing young people taking an interest in quilting."

"What will you be doing today?"

"I want these kids to walk away from the last class with a completely finished product. They are each going to make a placemat that they can use at home. We'll talk about choosing fabric, and I'll bring your box of fat quarters into the room so they can each choose three. After they make their choices, we'll read the pattern together and then use the rotary cutter to cut two of their fat quarters into two-and-a-half-inch strips.

"In the next class, they'll sew their strips together after they get familiar with the machine and the quarter-inch seam. The young students should have a completed top by the end of the second class.

"In the last class, we'll stack their tops with batting and backing and do some simple straight-line quilting. I haven't decided what to do about the binding yet. I need to see what these kids are capable of first."

"I like your plan," Ruth said. "The kids will leave here understanding the parts of a quilt and how it goes together, and they'll have a finished product to show off. Perhaps they'll come back for more advanced classes."

"That's what I hope. I'm designing a follow-up class to offer in case they're interested."

"Has there been any progress in the investigation?" Ruth asked. "I get at least one call a day from our quilters, asking what the police are doing."

"According to Charles, they seem to be at an impasse. These guys left no clues at all, but I know they're doing background checks on the custodial staff and even the guys who installed the frames and helped with hanging the quilts."

"Oh, that reminds me," Ruth said. "I need to get checks in the mail to those young men. I promised to pay them for their work, and it isn't their fault they didn't get to finish the job."

"Let's hope not," Sarah commented. She had been suspicious of the crew from the beginning. "I keep wondering why they were so eager to do the job, and that was before you offered to pay them. And did you notice how that one guy kept walking around like he was casing the joint the day he came to check out the room?"

"Casing the joint? You read too many mysteries, Sarah!" Ruth chuckled. "I think he was taking measurements and planning the placement of the frames."

"Well, I'm not the only one suspicious of them. Charles is looking into their backgrounds and doing some interviews over in Hamilton. It would have been very easy for them to plan the heist during their visits here."

"Plan the heist?" Ruth hooted. "You're really on a roll!"

"Well, what would you call it?" Sophie inquired as she walked into the room. She was there to help Sarah with the class. "You've heard of a diamond heist," she added. "This was a quilt heist, pure and simple."

"Enough of this," Ruth said, throwing up her arms in defeat. "It's time to open the shop, and your kids will be here in fifteen minutes. I'll get the coffeepot going."

"And cookies," Sophie called out. "Don't forget milk and cookies."

The class was a great success. At the end of the session, everyone wrote their name on a paper bag and filled it with their six carefully cut strips, the uncut fat quarter they had chosen for the back of their placemat, and a spool of coordinating thread.

"Just set them in this box," Sarah instructed, "and I'll keep them in the supply room until next week." The children were giggling and teasing each other as they left to meet their parents in the main shop.

"Mom, guess what we did," Sarah heard more than one child saying excitedly.

"Are you sure you charged enough for this class?" Sarah asked once the last student had left. "You're paying me and providing all these fat quarters and thread."

"It's not that much, and if it results in a few more quilters in the world, it's worth every penny."

"We'll see you tomorrow night," Sarah said as she pulled on her coat and turned to hurry Sophie along.

"I'm glad she didn't cancel the meeting," Sophie said as they approached their cars. "Let's tell the group about today's class. It's an uplifting topic, and quilters always love it when they hear about children learning to quilt."

"You're right about that! See you tomorrow."

* * * * *

"I wasn't sure if I wanted to come tonight," Kimberly was saying when Sarah and Sophie arrived at Running Stitches the next evening. "But Christina insisted."

Kimberly and Christina were sisters who did most of the long-arm quilting for the group. Their rates were reasonable. "Too reasonable," Sarah frequently told them. Between the two sisters, they had five quilts in the show, all made by their grandmother while her husband was away in the Second World War. "Lots of tears were shed over those quilts," Christina said, still remembering the stories her mother told about sitting under the frame while her mother quilted. "Granddad died over there, and I think that quilting frame kept Nana going."

"I don't know who made mine," Mabel said. In her late eighties, she was their oldest member and probably the most productive. She brought a large tote bag to every meeting filled with her latest accomplishments, all intended for her dozens of great-grandchildren. Her latest quilts were made for the new twin boys who were her great-great-grandchildren. "I got an early start," she had said jokingly when the group expressed astonishment that she had great-great-grandchildren.

Sarah and Sophie were the only ones without quilts in the show, but their hearts ached for the losses their friends had suffered, particularly Andy.

"Sarah," Ruth began. "Would you like to tell the group what you were doing yesterday?"

Sarah launched into a lively description of the fun she had had with the young quilters-to-be, and, as always, Sophie was able to interject just the right comments to get the group shedding tears of laughter.

By the time they broke for coffee and dessert, spirits were high, and they were beginning to talk about their next projects.

"It was a good meeting," Sarah said as she and Sophie drove home together.

"It was," Sophie agreed. "And an important meeting to have. Our friends needed a place to share their pain. But I think soon they are going to need reassurance that something is being done to locate the quilts. Do you think Detective Halifax or even Charles would be willing to come to the next meeting and talk about their progress?"

"That's an excellent idea. We don't meet for another two weeks, and that might be enough time for something positive to have come up in the investigation."

Chapter 18

"You volunteered me to do *what*?"

"All you have to do is go to the ladies' quilt club meeting, Hal. I know it's not your usual thing, but these nice people need to hear that something is being done."

"And why can't you do it, Charlie?" Hal asked. "You're the one who wants to be involved."

"Because I'm not official. You are the only one who can speak for the department. They want to know that you and your people are taking this as seriously as any other crime."

"As serious as a murder?" Hal retorted. "Or a hit-and-run? As serious as I took that guy who broke into the nursing home and wiped out their supply of drugs?"

Charles sighed. "Yes, I guess I am asking you to go talk to the women and explain that you're taking their loss just as seriously as everyone else's loss. It's only right, Hal. The quilts that these women lost were made by their mothers and grandmothers. Even their great-grandmothers. Didn't you have a grandmother, Hal?"

"Actually," Hal responded, "I have no idea."

Charles was immediately sorry he had let his impatience take over. His friend Hal had grown up in the foster care system and hadn't known his parents. "Sorry, Hal. I didn't mean …"

"It's okay. And I'll go speak to them next week. I don't know what I can say, but perhaps something will come up in the next few days."

"Actually, Sarah might have something for you by then. It's a long shot, but she saw an ad in a quilters' newsletter about antique quilts being sold at a quilt shop in Hamilton."

"That's not so unusual, is it?"

"Actually, it is. This particular shop doesn't carry antique quilts, just fabric, so this is something new. Sarah knows the shop owner, and she and Sophie are going over this week to look at the quilts on the unlikely chance that some of them are from the show."

"That's more than unlikely, Charlie. No one in their right mind would advertise the sale of stolen merchandise a few weeks after it was pinched and so close to where it was stolen."

* * * * *

"Come on, Sophie. We need to get on the road."

Sarah had read about the shop in Hamilton that was selling antique quilts, but she had been reluctant to check it out. Sarah had met the owner at a quilt show and had liked her. It was hard to imagine that she could be dealing in stolen merchandise.

A few days later, something happened to change Sarah's mind. A neighbor called and told Sarah that she had gone to the sale at the Hamilton shop, and she thought she saw some of the same quilts that had been on display at the show in the Village.

"We have to check this out," Sarah had announced, and Sophie, never one to miss an adventure, agreed to go with her.

"I'm getting worried," Sophie said as she climbed into Sarah's car. "This could be dangerous, and Charles should be with us."

"I didn't want Charles with us until we had a chance to look for ourselves, Sophie. Ruth is a good friend of the shop owner, and I don't want Charles causing the police to burst in on her. We'll just take a look and leave, okay? The woman who told us about the quilts isn't a quilter herself, and I'm sure similar quilts can look alike if you aren't familiar with all the varieties of patterns."

"I get it, I suppose," Sophie responded. "But I wish I had my gun with me."

"Sophie, you don't have a gun."

"I *could* have a gun," Sophie announced defiantly.

"I know, but you don't, and even if you did, we wouldn't be using it. You don't shoot people for possibly having stolen quilts."

"I would."

Sarah decided to drop the subject. Her friend was in a prickly mood and would best be left alone.

The two women were quiet for a few miles until Sophie called out suddenly, "There's that diner we like so much. Can we stop? I haven't had breakfast."

Ah, so that's the problem, Sarah thought with relief. Her friend could become exasperating when she was hungry.

"Great idea," Sarah responded as she pulled into the far left lane and sped across the oncoming lanes the moment there was a lull in the traffic.

They both relaxed once the waitress brought their coffee and pumpkin pancakes, a specialty at that time of the year. While they were eating, Sarah brought up the topic of the stolen quilts again, saying, "We need to plan what we'll do if we do see one of our quilts at the shop."

"True," Sophie responded, adding syrup to her tall stack.

"I think we should try to get a picture of it and just leave."

"I agree," Sophie said, wiping syrup from her chin with a napkin she had dampened in her water glass. Since there didn't seem to be disagreement any longer, Sarah relaxed and enjoyed her short stack.

An hour later, as they were walking toward the shop, Sarah stopped short and exclaimed, "Tessa! Tessa Livingstone! Thank goodness, I just remembered her name."

"And who is Tessa Livingstone?" Sophie asked with her eyebrows creeping up her forehead.

"The owner of the shop and Ruth's friend. I met her at the quilt show in Chicago a couple of years ago."

"Oh my," Sophie responded. "That's when Ruth was kidnapped. I'm sure glad I missed that show."

"Does Tessa sell fabric or just quilts?" Sophie asked as they approached the door.

"Oh, it's mainly a fabric shop, but she carries a few new quilts and vintage machines, I think."

"Like my little Featherweight?" Sophie asked excitedly.

"I think so, but very few quilts. This was the first time I've noticed antique quilts specifically mentioned in her ad."

"And that's what made you want to check it out?"

"Just a whim, Sophie. I thought it was strange that she suddenly had antique quilts, and it can't hurt to check it out.

It gets us into a new quilt shop, and that's always a good thing."

They stopped at the window for a few moments to admire the attractive display of new batik fabrics. As they entered the store, the woman standing behind the cutting table looked up and cried, "Sarah? Sarah Parker?"

"I'm surprised you remember me," Sarah responded as she walked over to the woman. They exchanged a friendly hug, and Sarah said, "It's good to see you, Tessa!"

"How's Ruth?" the shopkeeper asked as her smile faded. "It's been so long since we've gotten together. We used to meet at least once a month, but lately we've both been so busy. Has she recovered from that nightmare in Chicago?"

"She's doing just fine, Tessa. The shop is thriving, and she has three teachers now, and the classrooms are filled most of the time. She's determined to make quilters out of every resident of Middletown." Sarah introduced Sophie, and the three women visited for a few minutes until Sophie said she'd like to look around.

"Make yourself at home," Tessa said. "Take a look at those antique quilts over there in the corner. And you two can ignore the *Don't touch* sign since you know how to handle quilts."

Sarah carefully lifted the first few quilts and examined the ones farther down in the pile. They came to two or three Amish quilts lying together, and they looked at each other wordlessly. They were Ruth's quilts. It wasn't until they dug a little deeper that Sophie suddenly screamed out, "It's Andy's quilt. Look. It's Andy's!"

Tessa was approaching the table. "What's the problem?" she asked innocently.

"You know perfectly well what the problem is," Sophie screamed. "You stole my friend's quilt, and you even stole your own friend's quilts. These are Ruth's, and this one belongs to my friend Andy!"

"Sophie," Sarah said softly, "take another look. Please. This isn't Andy's quilt."

"Well, it …" she began. "Oh," she added as she lifted a corner and looked at the back. "Okay, so that one isn't Andy's, but those are Ruth's," she added stubbornly.

"What's going on here?" Tessa asked.

"I'm sorry, Tessa. It was a mistake. Come on, Sophie. We need to go." They headed for the door with Sarah practically dragging an objecting Sophie.

"Please wait, Sarah," Tessa pleaded. "I need to know what's going on. I just bought those quilts, and if they're stolen, I need to know it. Please stay and tell me what's going on."

"First, I want to talk to my husband," Sarah said as she pulled out her cell phone and called. "Where are you?" she asked, knowing that Charles had planned to do some shopping and said he might need to go to Hamilton to find what he needed.

"I'm in Hank's Hardware up in Hamilton. What's up?"

"I need you to come to the quilt shop right away. It's an emergency."

"It'll take me an hour. …"

"No, the quilt shop here in Hamilton. Sophie and I are here. We're on Main Street—509, I think."

"That's right," Tessa said in the background.

"I'll be there in ten minutes," Charles responded.

While they were waiting for Charles, Sarah began telling Tessa about the robbery, but Tessa immediately said that she knew about it. "Everyone in the quilting community knows about that," Tessa added. "It was a terrible thing to happen. All those poor people lost family memories. Wait! Are you saying ...?"

"Wait until my husband gets here."

Sophie didn't speak up, still angry about finding what she thought were stolen quilts in the shop. Sarah and Tessa went back to the table, and Sarah pulled out her cell phone with pictures of most of the stolen quilts. She shared the images with Tessa, who immediately said, "That one is on the pile. That one too," she exclaimed. "What's going on here?"

By the time Charles arrived, they had identified seven of the quilts that were stolen from the Cunningham Village quilt show. Tessa had been in the process of explaining where she had gotten them, and she started over for Charles' benefit.

"The guy was young and sort of scruffy looking. He wasn't your typical antique dealer, and when I asked about that, he said he procured antiques for his boss, and if I wanted to buy any of them instead, it would save him having to ship them. When I paid him for the seven quilts, he looked happy to see cash and stuffed it in his pocket. I did wonder why he didn't attempt to keep it separate from his own money, but some people aren't that organized."

Tessa was frantic when she realized she had inadvertently been offering stolen merchandise for sale. "We need to report this to the police right away," she announced to Sophie's surprise.

"I've already alerted them," Charles announced. "Tell them what you told us, and you'll probably have to account for how you obtained the other quilts, but you'll be cleared in the long run, I'm sure."

When the police arrived, one of the older officers immediately recognized Charles from his days on the force. "Charlie! What are you doing here?"

Charles explained to the officers what had happened, and the younger one spoke up, saying, "That kid is at it again. He's part of a gang that's making us crazy. There's no rhyme or reason to where they hit or what kind of merchandise they're after. This is the first time we caught them selling stuff instead of stealing it."

As they continued to talk, Tessa collected the paperwork she had on the other purchases. The younger officer pulled on the frayed edge of one of the older quilts and said, "You mean these old things are worth money?"

Sophie, immediately insulted, straightened up to her almost five feet height and said, "Don't touch that! Quilts have feelings, you know."

The officer backed away.

Once the officers were finished at the crime scene, Tessa was told to close the shop, and all four were taken to the police station to be interrogated individually. They were released hours later, exhausted and eager to go home. "May we take the seven quilts that belong to us?" Sophie asked.

"Sorry, miss. They are evidence," the officer responded. "We'll be holding them until the investigation is complete."

"At least we know where they are," Sarah said as she and Sophie drove home behind Charles.

"I'm going to call Charles," Sophie announced, "and see if he wants to stop for dinner at the diner, okay?"

"Great plan. This morning I saw that chicken pot pie was the special tonight, and we all need a dose of comfort food."

Chapter 19

"What did you learn from Hamilton PD?" Charles asked a few days later as he sat in Detective Halifax's office, sipping what the department fondly referred to as coffee. It hadn't changed in the many years since Charles had been sitting in this very office, despite the newer coffeepots.

"They've been after this gang for several years," the detective began. "It seems to be a bunch of young guys without much skill and no obvious leader. I don't know why they can't catch them, but they don't seem to follow any pattern."

"A gang?" Charles asked.

"Not exactly. They seem to be working independently. They work for someone out of town who will take most anything they can get, from fine art to those ragged old quilts."

"Don't let my wife hear you say that," Charles objected. "Those 'ragged old quilts' are like family to the people who treasure them. Many of the ones in the show were made in the 1800s. Can you imagine a piece of hand-stitched cloth lasting that many years?"

Hal looked at him like he was a stranger. "What's with you, Charlie? You getting soft?"

"And that's another thing," Charles said emphatically. "I haven't been Charlie since I left the force a decade ago. If you wouldn't mind, please call me Charles like everyone else."

"Sorry, Charlie … I mean Charles. I didn't know. Matt always called you Charlie."

"I know," Charles responded, suddenly looking sad. "Originally, I objected because I was always Charlie on the job, and I wanted to start a new life after I retired, but later when Matt was the only person left who called me Charlie … well, now hearing it reminds me that old Matt is gone."

Both men remained silent for a while, each lost in his own memories of Lieutenant Matthew Stokely. Matt had been Charles' lieutenant for many years as well as his closest friend. Matt was there when Charles' first wife died, and when Matt's wife, Doris, was tragically killed, Charles was there. For the past year, Charles had grieved the loss of Matt himself.

Young Halifax, on the other hand, came to Lieutenant Stokely as a new recruit and immediately saw in the man the father he had never had. Matt took on the responsibility willingly, never having had a son himself.

"Okay, let's deal with this quilt show issue," Charles began. "Hamilton PD has been after these small-time crooks for two years with no luck."

"Oh, they've caught a few of them. They can describe how it goes down, but they don't know who the bosses are. They send the merchandise to them by truck."

"They arranged for a truck? Where does it go?" Charles asked.

"No, they don't have anything to do with getting the truck. It's delivered to them as soon as they have enough to make it worthwhile. They call a number that changes weekly. They meet the truck where they are told, and they load it. They couldn't charge any of the guys with much because they never got their hands on the stolen goods. The merchandise was long gone."

"Are you saying that the boss, or bosses, are running this from out of town? Not the mob, I assume."

"Nah. Too penny-ante for the mob."

"You mentioned priceless antiques," Charles reminded him.

"Yeah, a few were lifted during estate sales. A lot of small stuff as well. These quilts now, I don't get. They can't be worth much."

"Begging to differ, my friend. I've been following online sales this week, and I've seen them range from $500 to $5,000, and there are probably some for more than that."

"How about the ones in the show? Are they worth that much?"

"The quilters estimated their average value at around $800, but I think they were underestimating the worth of some of the oldest ones."

"We believe this is the first time they've hit Middletown, assuming it's the same guys, but we're going back and looking at some of our open cases. Hamilton has sent the word out to other cities, and it seems to be going on all over the Upper Midwest. No telling where else they're operating."

"Where do you suppose this stuff is ending up?"

"No idea. Hamilton found a few pieces in California and New Mexico."

"How did they find them?" Charles asked.

"Internet sales."

"Ah. Good idea. So what do you think, Hal? Is this information that you could share with Sarah's quilt group? They need to hear that something is being done."

"Yeah, I'll give them an abbreviated version of what we talked about. Do you suppose these old ladies are computer savvy?"

"First of all, they aren't 'old ladies.' " Charles hesitated and added, "Well, some are, but that sounds pretty harsh. My wife is one of them, you know."

"I'd hardly call Sarah an 'old lady,' " Hal responded with a chuckle.

"So, what's your point, Hal?" Charles asked, trying to hold back his irritation.

"What I was leading up to was whether any of these women could do computer searches and see if they saw their own quilts online anywhere."

"Hmm. Not a bad idea, but on the other hand, who would be dumb enough to advertise stolen merchandise online so soon after stealing it?"

"That could be true of some rare items, but these guys might think that no one would be searching for quilts that way."

"Because they probably belong to little old ladies?" Charles responded sarcastically.

"Okay, I get it. I apologize to you and Sarah and all the women in the quilt club," the detective said, holding his hands up in acquiescence.

"Okay, that's something you could introduce to the women when you speak to them next week, and they might at least feel like they are doing something. In the meantime, I intend to get on the computer myself and learn where old quilts get listed."

"Good idea. Let me know if you come up with anything."

* * * * *

"Okay, Sophie, I'm ready to take a closer look at this scooter of yours."

Sophie began to dismount her fire-engine red mobility scooter, but Sarah adamantly objected.

"No, no! I don't want to ride it. I just want to look at it."

"Well, you can appreciate it more by sitting in it. You won't believe how comfortable it is."

"But I'm not ready to ride in it," Sarah insisted.

"I know. Just sit down." Sophie moved aside, and Sarah easily slipped onto the seat.

"Wow. This is comfortable," she remarked, looking surprised. She spread her arms out on the padded armrests and sat back in the seat. "Really comfortable," she repeated. "And you can drive it on the roads?"

"You can here in the Village, but in town you have to stay on the sidewalk. I only want it for here, but Norman said we might take it to Kentucky when we go to his cabin in the spring. I can drive it around in the park. He said it's good on grass and gravel. Even rough terrain."

"How fast can it go?"

"I've only gone a few miles an hour, but Norman said it could go up to fifteen miles an hour. I know that's not very fast, but it's fine for tooling around here in the Village, and it's hard for me to walk on rough terrain like they have in the Land Between the Lakes."

"What're these switches for?"

"Headlights and turn signals," Sophie responded expertly. "Norman went over the whole thing with me. I wasn't sure I wanted to keep it, but it's convenient for going to the Center or just driving around the community. Besides, it's fun. Don't you want to try it?"

"I guess I will. I'll just go around the edge of our cul-de-sac," Sarah decided. "How do I start it?"

"Just like a car. Turn the key."

Sarah started the scooter and suddenly squealed, "How do I make it go? There aren't any pedals."

"The speed control lever is on your handle. Squeeze it to move and for more speed."

"Where's the lever for stopping?"

"You use the same lever, Sarah. Just let up on it to slow down and stop."

"It must take a while to get used to that," Sarah said as she tried moving a few feet forward and then stopping."

"It doesn't take long. Just go really slow."

"I think I'll go all the way down to the entrance to our street," Sarah said once she had traveled five or six feet at about one mile an hour."

"Okay, but pick up your speed just a little," Sophie suggested as she walked by Sarah's side.

"I don't want to go any faster than you can walk," Sarah responded. "I want you by me."

"Nonsense," Sophie responded. "You're the brave one in this group. Get going. I'll wait for you in front of your house."

Sophie watched as Sarah finally reached the end of the block and turned to return to her cul-de-sac. Sophie noticed that her friend stopped the scooter and walked it around until it was facing home. But she hopped right back on and traveled much faster coming back home. She pulled into the driveway with a broad smile. "That was a blast."

"I knew you'd like it," Sophie responded. "By the way, how about that chili and cornbread dinner you promised? I'm starving."

"It's all made and will only take a short time in the oven once we get in."

Norman and Charles had been looking at private quilt sales on the internet, but once they realized what was going on out front, they decided to watch from the living room window.

"You drove that thing like a professional," Charles kidded as Sarah walked in the door.

"You were watching?" she replied, looking embarrassed. "I never got it over five miles an hour."

"Are you going to want one?" Charles asked with a twinkle in his eye.

"Absolutely not," she responded emphatically. She wondered about that look. *I hope he isn't planning to surprise me with one*, she thought. "And if I ever change my mind, I'll let you know," she added.

The men returned to the computer room, and Sophie and Sarah poured themselves a glass of wine. Sophie sat at the kitchen table and watched as Sarah transferred her Crock-Pot full of chili into a rectangular glass baking dish. She then removed a pitcher from the refrigerator that contained a thick yellow mixture.

"What's that?" Sophie asked.

"That's our cornbread. I had it all mixed and ready to bake," Sarah responded as she carefully poured the mixture over the chili.

"You're baking it on top of the chili?"

"The best way to do it. You'll see."

After dinner, the two friends retired to the sewing room and spent the rest of the evening planning the quilt they were going to make as a fundraiser for the local women's shelter.

"Will you be asking the quilt group to make some of the blocks?" Sophie asked.

"I think you and I can make this one together. It's a simple pattern, and I'd like to get it to our quilter right away so we can deliver it to the shelter before their winter fundraiser."

Sarah pulled out her containers of yellow and blue fabrics, and they chose a variety of pieces in both colors for their scrap quilt. "I'll cut these into strips tonight, and we can start sewing tomorrow."

"I'll be here by 10:00," Sophie responded as she stood to leave. "Norman wants to get me home early tonight so that he can go home and pack for his trip to Chicago."

"Event planners' convention, right?"

"That's right. He's retired, but I think Norman is probably as involved as he was before he retired."

"Did you think about going with him?"

"He asked, but I wanted him to do this by himself. I think it's important that we both continue to enjoy our own interests."

"I agree," Sarah responded. She and Charles enjoyed their time together, but they each had their own hobbies and interests as well.

"Do you really think we can finish the quilt tomorrow?" Sophie asked as she was putting on her coat. She had found the book of patterns in a thrift shop, and it was entitled *Quilt in a Day.*

"I guess we'll find out," Sarah responded doubtfully.

Chapter 20

Ruth introduced Detective Halifax, although he had met most of the club members at the Parkers' house the day after the theft. He told the group that he was there to let them know what progress had been made in the investigation.

Detective Halifax cleared his throat and began. "Good evening, ladies." He then paused. He had intended to ask Charles what to call the members of this group. He had trouble keeping up with what was politically correct at any given moment. He had the feeling that "ladies" was the wrong term, and once he looked around and saw a young man in the audience, he knew he had made the wrong choice for yet another reason.

"I wanted to let you folks know what we've learned." Feeling a bit more comfortable once he saw friendly smiles of encouragement, he went on to explain about the quilts that had been located in Hamilton. He assured the owners of those seven quilts that the quilts would be returned to them at the end of the investigation.

"Where are they now?" one of the women asked.

"They are being held by the Hamilton Police Department, and I've been assured that they have been packaged and stored safely following proper procedures."

"They know how to store valuable quilts?" someone else called out.

"They contacted Mrs. Weaver here," he said, looking toward Ruth, "who is the owner of several of the quilts being held, and she informed them about storage."

"Thank you," the person responded.

"They haven't been able to apprehend the man involved, but I've been assured that it's high priority. They are treating our crime here in the Village as part of an ongoing investigation in Hamilton involving several similar thefts."

"As for here in Middletown, we have a couple of suspects. I'm not at liberty to discuss the details, but rest assured we are taking this very seriously."

"I've seen the police chief on television," Sophie said as she stood, "and he's telling people to call in if they know anything about the crime. Do you get calls, and have any of them provided useful information?"

"Again, I'm not at liberty to discuss details of those calls, but I can tell you that two of those calls led us to our current suspects. We may, in fact, be making an arrest shortly."

"Do you think we'll get the rest of the quilts back?" Sophie added before sitting down.

"I can't answer that definitively, but if the theft here is related to the ones in Hamilton, they believe the merchandise is being shipped to other states for sale. If that's true, it would be tough to recover them. And that brings me to something I wanted to discuss with you."

Detective Halifax reached for the glass of water that had been thoughtfully provided on his makeshift podium. "I would like to request that everyone who knows how to access the internet begin searching for your quilts. If you find one, however, please do nothing. Call me immediately, and I'll check it out. Contacting them yourself could cause us to lose the suspect and the quilt or quilts he might have."

"How do we do these searches?" someone asked.

"Do searches on images of antique or vintage quilts for sale and keep going through them until you, hopefully, find a familiar one. When you do, simply write down the URL and call me."

"What's a URL?" the young man in the back asked.

"It's the computer address of the website posting the ad." The young man looked confused, but Ruth immediately came to his aid.

"I'll show you, Frank. In fact, you and I can do that here in the shop. I have pictures of all the quilts, and we'll especially look for your grandmother's." She gave the detective a sorrowful look. "He lost all of his grandmother's quilts, some from the early 1800s."

The detective looked pained and shook his head. Looking up at the young man, he said, "Sorry, sir."

"I don't have much else to report," the detective said. "I want you to know we take your losses very seriously, and we'll continue to work this case until we've covered every possibility. I can only say that I sincerely hope we can recover your quilts."

Moving to the front of the room, Ruth said, "We want to thank you, Detective Halifax, for taking the time to come talk to us. We know you're a busy man, but it's meant a great deal to us to hear how serious you are about helping us."

Everyone clapped as he moved toward the door to leave, but then he stopped and reached into his pocket. "Here is a pile of my cards. Call me directly if you find anything online."

"We will," several people called out enthusiastically.

"I can't wait to get to my computer," Sophie said. "This will be fun, and just think how many quilts we're going to see."

"I just want to see ours," Christina said.

* * * * *

"Yes," Charles responded when Sarah told him about Hal's request for the quilters to do computer searches. "He asked me if I thought the group would do that, and I thought they'd be eager to get involved."

"You were right. Not everyone has a computer, but the younger ones were particularly eager. Sophie could hardly wait to get home to try it out."

At that moment the phone rang.

"Can Charles come help me? I keep getting an error message when I try to search for the quilts."

"It's getting pretty late, my friend," Sarah responded with a chuckle. "Go to bed, and tomorrow we'll do this together. I'll come over after breakfast, okay?"

"Okay. But do you know how to do it?"

"I might be able to, but I'll try it out here before I come so Charles can help if I'm doing it wrong." She smiled at her husband, who knew she could do computer searches with her eyes closed, but he appreciated how her comment supported her friend Sophie's efforts. "See you in the morning," Sarah said as she hung up.

"How did Hal do?" Charles asked.

"Well, at first he seemed nervous, but once he got going, he did fine. He didn't tell us anything we didn't know, but he was reassuring. I think getting the members involved in searching the internet will help them. I know they feel helpless right now, and participating in the investigation might help them feel more in control. But the truth is, we may never see any of those quilts again."

"Wait a minute," Charles responded. "We have seven of them back, twenty-nine to go. We just might start chipping away at that number. I'm planning to spend all day tomorrow on the internet myself. Leave me a copy of the quilt pictures when you go to Sophie's tomorrow."

"By the way, Charles, Hal said tonight they have a couple of suspects. What's that all about?"

"Oh, I forgot to tell you, mainly because it's not at all promising. But one of the guys Ruth's friend sent over to set up the frames has disappeared. A couple of Hal's men accompanied Hamilton PD, and they found the guy's apartment empty. The landlord said he moved out several weeks ago, not long after the robbery."

"Do they know where he went?"

"No one knows, but Hamilton PD is following up with neighbors and the people he worked with through the quilt guild. Someone must know where he went."

"Will Hamilton take this seriously?"

"Absolutely, because they see what happened here as part of a larger scheme and one they've been trying to solve for themselves."

"Oh yes," Sarah acknowledged. "Hal said something about that tonight, and the investigators at Tessa's shop seemed to think the crimes are all connected."

"Hal said they've identified two suspects. Who's the other one?"

"Well," Charles replied with a frown, "that's the one I don't like. They're looking at Lonnie."

"Lonnie Dunkin, the maintenance supervisor? Why would they be looking at him?"

"He had opportunity, and he's got a shady background, Sarah. His brother is in prison for murder. Lonnie and I've been friends since his brother's trial, and I know he's a good guy, but his record doesn't look good. He's been in some trouble over the years."

"You got him that job, didn't you?"

"I sure did, and I'd do it again. He's a good man."

"I hate to say this, Charles, but you thought his brother was a good man too, and he let you sit in jail for weeks for a crime he committed."

"I know, Sarah. I know."

"Let's put this aside for now and go to bed," she said. "Tomorrow is another day."

Charles chuckled and said, "Okay, Scarlett. You're right." He switched off the kitchen light, and the two walked arm in arm toward their room.

Chapter 21

"Sophie, I got great news today from *Quilters' News Quarterly*."

"Who are they?"

"They are one of the publications I contacted about printing my article about our quilts. Ruth told me about them. They're nationwide, and this is something they do regularly. They called this morning, and they want to write their own version of our story and feature it in their next publication along with all the pictures. The woman I spoke to said they've been very successful in recovering lost and stolen quilts over the years."

"That's terrific," Sophie responded. "How will this work? Do you have to go somewhere?"

"Their main office is in Paducah, and they're sending a reporter up to interview us, and …"

"Wait, did you say 'us'?" Sophie gasped.

"I'd like for you to be with me, and I think we should have Ruth, too."

"And maybe Andy," Sophie suggested. "His story is unique since his daughter just recently found their only relative, and that quilt has a special history."

"We can ask him. The story is pretty personal, but he'd be a good addition to the meeting with the reporter. Charles, too, I think."

"I wonder if Detective Halifax might be willing to be interviewed," Sophie said.

"Charles can ask him. He wouldn't have to be at our meeting. They could just go see him to find out what the police are doing."

"So when is this reporter coming?" Sophie asked.

"Friday," Sarah responded. "I've got a lot of organizing to do before then. So," she added, "you'll come?"

"I'll be there with bells on."

"Leave the bells home, my friend. We need to treat this interview with dignity."

* * * * *

At 2:00 on Friday afternoon, when Sarah opened the door to the reporter, she was stunned by the crowd on the porch. A rather distinguished-looking man stepped forward and introduced himself as Todd Manchin, the editor of the publication. Sarah hadn't expected them to send their editor. He then introduced Susan Lake, his lead reporter, and her assistant, John Waterford. Standing in the back was a rather scruffy-looking guy loaded down with camera equipment. He was introduced as Lance-the-Cameraman.

Once the visitors joined Sarah and her friends, the living room was filled. Charles brought in a few more chairs from the dining room, and Sophie added glasses to the coffee table, which had been set up with a pitcher of tea and several plates of cookies.

Sarah began by telling the story of the quilt show and how it had come about. She then passed out pictures that had been taken during the show. "I have an individual picture of each quilt as well, which you can take with you," she explained.

"We'd like to use some of these pictures from the show as well," Todd said. "They set the scene."

Then Sarah asked Charles if he would talk to them about what had happened the night of the robbery and what the police had been able to do so far. The detective, unfortunately, wasn't available to be interviewed. "It's more likely that his boss didn't want the publicity," Charles had observed earlier that day.

Charles told the group what he could about the police investigation, and Sarah interjected things the detective had told them at the recent meeting.

Turning to his wife, Charles asked, "Did you tell them about the other articles you sent out?"

"Only briefly," she replied. Then to the group, she added, "I'm not a writer, but I submitted articles to all the quilt magazines I could find and also to quilt shops that have catalogs. I told our story pretty much like I told it to you, and I included all the pictures. Only one responded so far, and they ran the article but only a few of the pictures."

"That's excellent, Sarah," Susan responded. "If anyone else offers to print your story, give them our website and tell them that all the pictures will be displayed there." Susan handed Sarah her card with the website address. "In fact, you might want to send an abbreviated version of the story to all of them again along with three or four pictures and give them our website for more information. They might go for something shorter."

Charles then told the group about his search efforts, and both Todd and Susan were able to give him several websites to search and a few pointers for making the most of his searches.

Sophie, to Sarah's surprise, was rather quiet, offering only a few comments now and then. Susan, the reporter, was very knowledgeable about quilts in general and the recovery of quilts in particular. "There's a good chance you'll get some of your quilts back, Sarah," she said. "Our publication is nationwide and reaches many people in the business of vintage and antique quilts. We also place all the quilt photos on our website, which reaches thousands of people all over the world."

"It's unlikely that our quilts have left the country," Sarah responded.

"Oh, I wouldn't be so sure. Quilts made during our Civil War period are trendy overseas."

After a couple of hours of discussion, taped interviews, and photographs by Lance-the-Cameraman, the visitors stood and thanked their hosts. "I'll probably be calling you," Susan said, "once I begin writing."

Todd and Susan passed out their cards and asked that they be contacted if anyone thought of anything else.

"Good luck with your computer searches, Charles. Keep us in the loop if you find anything promising or if we can help in any way," Todd called out over his shoulder as the group progressed across the porch and down the steps.

Once everyone was gone except Sophie, Charles brought a cold bottle of chardonnay into the living room, and the three friends put their feet up to relax. "Well, what do you think?" Sarah asked.

"I think I'm getting on the computer again tomorrow morning, but I think our best leads will come from the article these folks put out there," Charles replied.

"I was astonished to hear how often they receive information from people who have seen the quilts they feature in their publication. They have a fair recovery rate. I'm beginning to feel hopeful for the first time," Sarah remarked.

"I wanted to ask something all afternoon, Sophie. You were very quiet today. Are you okay?" Charles asked, looking concerned.

"I'm fine. Your wife told me to leave my bells at home, so I did."

Charles looked confused, but Sarah burst out laughing and said, "Sophie, you are always welcome with bells on. Your bells bring smiles to everyone."

Charles, still looking confused, muttered, "What bells?"

Chapter 22

The article had been completed and was expected to be online later in the day. Print copies were in the mail but hadn't arrived in Middletown yet.

Hal had brought Lonnie Dunkin, the Community Center facilities manager, into the department twice in one week for further interrogation. He hadn't made an arrest, but Charles was afraid he was close to doing just that. He learned that Lonnie had, without authorization, arranged to have the locks changed the morning after the quilts were taken and had thrown out the old locks, which were now unavailable to the crime lab.

"The crime tape was up, Charles," Hal said heatedly. "Despite that, the man destroyed evidence and interfered in the investigation. Why do you suppose he didn't want us seeing those locks?" he asked, not expecting an answer.

"You're making assumptions, Hal. Lonnie said he was afraid the thieves had keys, and he wanted the building secured. That's one of his responsibilities."

"Well, we'll never know now, will we?"

The two men remained silent, but both were seething.

"He hasn't been charged yet, has he?" Charles finally asked.

"Not yet, but we're close."

"What about the other suspects? Why are you closing in on Lonnie Dunkin? What about that Hamilton guy who hung the quilts and then vanished from the face of the earth? What about him?"

"There's not one scrap of evidence that he was involved."

"His fingerprints were all over the frames," Charles responded impatiently.

"He hung the quilts, Charles. He hung the quilts, and then he moved. Those are not crimes."

"He suddenly moved right after the quilts were stolen, and he had opportunity," Charles announced.

"How's that?" Hal asked. "You and your wife let him out of the building and locked the door behind him, right?"

"He could have come back. . . ." Charles began, but then remembered the problem with the locks being changed. "Okay, so let me ask about the woman we brought in who saw someone lurking around in the bathroom when the show was closing. She was certainly suspicious, and the woman we brought in was able to give you a detailed description of the woman, assuming it was really a woman," he added.

"She had the sketch artist draw a picture alright, but it wasn't of any criminal."

"Who was it?"

"It was the mayor's wife."

"What?" Charles was clearly shocked.

"You can't tell anyone what I'm about to tell you, not even Sarah."

Charles looked offended, and Hal revised his statement. "Okay, you can tell Sarah, but no one else. First of all, the mayor's wife has a full-time caregiver due to her condition, and he doesn't want anyone to know."

"Her condition?"

"I'll spell it out for you," the detective said with a sigh. "There's some dementia there, and this is top secret. The mayor doesn't want the press getting ahold of that information. But the fact is, she can't be left alone. The mayor thought she'd enjoy the quilt show, and he arranged for her caregiver to accompany her. Something happened, and the details aren't even being shared with us, but they got separated. That was the mayor's wife that your friend Myra described to the sketch artist. At closing time, Lonnie checked the bathrooms and found her. He recognized her right away and whisked her out of the Center and drove her home."

"Lonnie did that?" Charles queried in a sardonic tone, with both eyebrows high on his forehead. "That must have been difficult while planning a major crime only moments later."

"Go home, Charlie," Hal responded, reverting to his previous habit of calling his friend by his nickname. "Just go home."

* * * * *

"Come look at the quilts I found online."

"Did you find one?" Sarah asked excitedly as she set down the pan she had been washing.

"Unfortunately, they aren't ours, but it's an incredible site with hundreds of quilts that have been reported as lost or stolen over the years. This is on the *Quilters' News Quarterly* website. They keep this registry of every quilt that has ever been reported to them as missing, and they don't remove it until it's found. It's fascinating to look at," he said as Sarah sat down at his computer and began scrolling through the pictures.

"It's fascinating and very sad," she responded. "I feel like I do when I look at animal rescue sites and see all those homeless animals. These quilts weren't exactly abandoned, but they were loved by someone, somewhere. I wonder if people know about these sites." Suddenly she stopped on a quilt with a gasp, but then said, "No, that's not it. I thought for a moment that was one of Mabel's, but her colors were faded, and the binding was frayed."

"Our pictures are in here, but they're up at the front. They put the newest ones at the top of the list. Scroll back the other way."

"Oh my," Sarah sighed sadly. "Here they are. It's so sad to see them listed as 'Missing or Stolen.' There are so many listed here. How will anyone notice ours?"

"This isn't the only place they are. They went out in the print version to their mailing list, and they're over here along with the article on the home page. Click here," Charles said, pointing to the icon for the home page.

ARTICLE:
Tragedy in Middletown—Loss of 36 Quilts

The article included pictures of Cunningham Village and the pictures taken during the quilt show. Then it shocked the viewer with an image of the same room, now empty. It went on to describe what had happened and the magnitude of the personal loss to the many quilters. The website then displayed each quilt individually and provided a phone number to call with any information.

"They listed John Waterford's number," Sarah remarked. "Do you think he knows enough about quilts to be doing this job?"

"Don't forget," Charles responded, "he works for Susan, and she certainly knows quilts. If she trusts him, I think we can too."

Chapter 23

The quilters had been sitting around in their meeting room for nearly an hour talking about the articles in the quilt magazines, the pictures of their quilts online, and their unsuccessful internet searches.

"This is depressing," Delores said suddenly. "We need another charity project to take our minds off the lost quilts." Everyone nodded their agreement. The group had completed 120 placemats for the Meals on Wheels program during the late summer, but, other than the show, they hadn't discussed another project since then.

"Does anyone have an idea?"

"I love making baby quilts," Myrtle said in her quiet voice. "As a matter of fact, I brought some that I've been working on for my great-grandsons. Twins, they are!"

Everyone clapped and asked to see the quilts.

"This is for Darnell," she said proudly, holding up the first of the quilts. "And this is for Tyrone. They only weighed a little over four pounds, but they're doing great. Their mama's going to have her hands full, though. She already had three young'uns, all boys," she added with a proud chuckle. "But we're all helping. We've got a big family."

The group passed the quilts around, handling them gently and with admiration. Myrtle did exquisite work. The group went on to discuss making baby quilts but decided to put that off for now since they had recently made children's quilts for the women's shelter.

"We could always do pillowcases for the shelter, but I made so many last Christmas that I'm really tired of making them," Delores complained.

"Any other ideas?" Ruth asked, but there was no response.

"Well, I have something to show the group," Ruth said, reaching into her tote bag. She held up what at first looked like a divided tote bag, but then Ruth held up the back, and they could see that it looked more like a miniature saddlebag that obviously went over something.

"What is it?" Frank asked. Frank was the club's only male member. He worked as a greeter at a local big-box store and loved sewing. Frank had initially gone into Running Stitches because of a table runner he saw in the window. He wanted to buy it for his grandmother; but Sarah, who happened to be in the shop, explained that it was a sample for a class she would be offering. She suggested he take the class and learn to make it. With help, Frank learned the basics and had recently completed a quilt for his bed. "Does it go over a horse?" he asked.

"Actually, it could if it were bigger, I suppose," Ruth said with a laugh, "but this is called a walker bag, and it attaches to the front of a walker. It gives the person a place to keep their things like their cell phone, a book, Kleenex, knitting, quilt projects—whatever they want to carry with them. Here," she added, reaching into her tote bag again. "I printed out this picture of a walker bag attached to a walker." She handed the picture to Frank to pass around.

"I get it," he exclaimed. "My grandma uses a walker sometimes. Are we going to make these? I want to make one for Grandma." He began to rock back and forth excitedly.

"We're going to talk about it right now," Ruth responded, laying her hand gently on Frank's shoulder, "but we can certainly make one for your grandmother," she added with a reassuring smile.

"Thank you," he said more calmly now. "Grandma will like that."

"This looks easy," Becky exclaimed after a careful examination. Becky had just joined the group after taking Sarah's Introduction to Quilting class. She was a skilled seamstress and had been sewing since she was in high school but had never learned to quilt. She became interested during her first visit to Ruth's shop, when she saw the beautiful quilts hanging on the walls.

"What would we do with them?" Allison asked. With Caitlyn gone, Allison was now the youngest member of the group.

"Nursing homes, perhaps," Delores said.

"Or maybe we could stop by the Senior Center and see if they would like some for their members."

"I like that idea," Becky said. "I volunteer there, and I see plenty of people using walkers, but I've never seen one with an attached bag. This would be really useful."

"If we had enough, we could even offer some to Meals on Wheels. That would be a way to reach people in the community," Allison suggested. Allison had been excited about the program and was now volunteering with them. "One lady I take meals to could sure use one. She's always asking me to find her remote control and cell phone when they slip down under her chair. She could keep them right by her in her walker bag. In fact, I think I'll make her one on my own."

"Well, folks," Ruth began. "With all the suggestions for who could use them, I think this means you like the idea?"

Everyone responded enthusiastically.

"Okay, there are several patterns online, but I think this one would be a good one for us to make. It can be made in an evening easily, and it has four nice pockets." She gave them the name of the site so everyone could order their own patterns. "Does everyone have access to the internet?"

"I don't, but one of my grandsons can do it for me," Myrtle responded.

"I don't have a computer or a grandson," Peggy announced. "Can I give my money to someone to do it for me?"

"Me, too," Frank said.

"We'll order them for anyone who doesn't have access to a computer," Kimberly and her sister Christina said almost in unison. "Just see one of us after the meeting."

"I made copies of the supply list so you can begin pulling together what you'll need. Let's plan to start working on this at our next meeting."

"I have a suggestion," Mabel said. "We only have a couple of meetings before Christmas, and we're probably all busy with gifts." There were numerous mumbled comments which boiled down to the fact that they all had too many projects and too little time.

"How about we order our patterns and get our fabric together, but we save this project until after the holidays," Ruth suggested.

There were lots of nods of agreement.

"But we definitely have to do this in January," Delores said. "I love the idea of the walker bags."

"It was good to see the group excited about something again," Sophie said as she and Sarah were driving home.

"And I think you and I should get back to our wall hangings. It's just a little over a month until Christmas," Sarah said, "and I want to make one for Jason and Jennifer, and I want to send one to Caitlyn for her room, and maybe another for her to give to her aunt. What do you think?"

"That works. I was going to make one for Andy and, of course, for Timmy and Martha. Oh, wait! Martha is your daughter. Did you want to make one for them?"

"Sophie, this whole thing was your idea. You're already making one for them. And remember, we were going to keep making holiday-themed ones for them, so maybe I can make the next one."

"That's fine. I love being sisters-in-law with you," Sophie responded.

"Is that what we are now? I was never able to figure that one out. But whatever we are, I love it too." She reached over and squeezed her friend's hand as she was getting out of the car.

* * * * *

"Hi, Aunt Sarah. How was your Thanksgiving?"

"The only thing missing was you," Sarah responded. "Did you and your aunt have a nice day?"

Caitlyn told Sarah about Maddie's friends who had come for the day. "They were mostly old, but this one woman brought her grandson. He's a little older than I am, but," Caitlyn added with a giggle, "he was so cute!"

"Really?" Sarah responded teasingly. "Just how cute?"

"Maybe the cutest guy I ever met," the young girl replied, still giggling.

"Did he ask you out?"

"Yes. He wants me to go to a movie this weekend."

"How much older is he?"

"Only three, maybe four years," she responded tentatively, "but you know …"

"Yeah, a few years can make a big difference when you're young. Do you think you should go out with him?"

"I told him I'd let him know today, but I can't decide whether to go or not."

"May I make a suggestion?"

"Of course!" Caitlyn responded eagerly. "That's why I called you. What should I do?"

"Well, I can't tell you that, but I can make a suggestion. How about inviting your friend Beth and her boyfriend to go along? We used to call it a 'double date' in the olden days," Sarah said with a smile in her voice. "I don't know if you still do."

"They are sort of young for Steven," Caitlyn responded.

"They are both your age, aren't they?"

"Well, yes."

"So?"

"I don't know. He might think I'm afraid to go out alone with him."

"Are you?"

"Not exactly, but …"

"Caitlyn, I'm beginning to think you already know what you should do. This older boy makes you feel uncomfortable."

"He does, but I think I shouldn't feel that way."

"Caitlyn, listen to your Aunt Sarah. You must always follow your instincts. You are a bright girl who got yourself through things no young girl should have to endure. You know what you should do."

"I should tell him no."

"I suspect that's exactly what you should do."

"Thank you, Aunt Sarah. And you're right. I was afraid he'd think I was some sort of naive kid, but it doesn't matter what he thinks, does it?"

"Not one iota."

"I've always wanted to ask someone: What's an iota?"

"That's an easier question to answer. I have absolutely no idea!" They both laughed.

As they were hanging up, Caitlyn suddenly said, "Wait, Aunt Sarah. I have it." Sarah could hear a few clicks and knew Caitlyn was on her computer. "It's the ninth letter of the Greek alphabet, and it means a very small amount."

"Well, that makes sense," Sarah responded.

They hung up laughing, with both feeling much relieved about the handsome grandson.

Chapter 24

"Sarah, if I ever get my aunt Maddie's quilt back, would you repair it for me?"

"Oh, Andy, I don't know anything about that. We should talk to Ruth. I'm sure she knows people who restore quilts. What is it you want to do?"

"I don't want to change it, but I'm concerned about those places where the fabric has disintegrated. The stuffing is coming out."

"Stuffing? Oh, you mean the batting. I noticed that too. If that's all you want to do, I think we could find some antique fabric, and I could appliqué over the disintegrated pieces."

"I don't know what that means," Andy replied with a frown.

"Here, let me show you. Sophie left her appliqué project here." Sarah was gone for a few minutes and returned with Sophie's project tote. She removed one of the wall hangings Sophie had been working on, and, fortunately, there was one petal that had only been appliquéd on one side. Sarah was able to lift the edge and show Andy how Sophie was stitching it down to the background.

"We'd do it just like this. We can go to a couple of antique shops and find some old fabric. I could cut the original shape and simply appliqué it down. Actually, it might be better to get Sophie involved in this since she's the appliqué expert."

When Charles entered the room, Andy and Sarah had fabric spread out on the living room floor, and Andy was pinning a small piece of fabric to a larger piece. "What in the world are you two doing? Sarah, what have you done to my friend?"

"It's okay, Charles," Andy responded, grunting as he pulled himself up off the floor. "She's showing me what she'll be doing to my quilt, and I'm just trying to understand. You see, she's offered to …"

"Give it up, Andy," Sarah interjected. "You'll just make his eyes twirl around. It happens whenever my husband is faced with fabric talk."

"Actually," Andy responded, suddenly looking despondent, "I guess I've been pretending that I was going to get my quilt back, but I should just accept the fact that it's gone."

"Did Hal have any news?" Sarah asked, knowing her husband had just met with the detective.

"Not good news. He's having Lonnie arrested this afternoon. I went by and asked Lonnie if he wanted me to wait with him, but he said he was going to turn himself in before they came for him."

"You mean it was Lonnie Dunkin, the facilities manager, all along?" Andy responded, looking shocked. "That's unbelievable."

"It's more than unbelievable, Andy. The guy had nothing to do with it. The department is way off base on this one."

"You know that for sure?" Andy asked.

"As sure as any of us can be about anything. I just know he couldn't have done it. He doesn't have it in him." As Charles spoke, he saw the look on Sarah's face and knew what she was thinking. *You've been wrong before about those two brothers.*

"For Lonnie's sake, we've got to figure out what happened to those quilts," Andy announced firmly. "Charles, are you in?"

"Sure! I've been in from the beginning."

"Sarah?"

"Yes, Andy, I'm in, and I can speak for Sophie. Let's go over to her house. She'll want to be near her card file." The three chuckled.

Once the three arrived at Sophie's, she immediately began making notes, as they knew she would.

"Okay, let's start with the woman in the ladies' room when the show was closing," Sophie said as she wrote on the first card.

"It wasn't her," Charles said. "Hal already eliminated her."

"And he did not eliminate Lonnie, so I'm not going to consider his opinions. He could be wrong."

Charles was torn about his promise to keep the mayor's wife out of the investigation but decided he could trust his friends.

He told what he knew, and Sophie simply said, "As I said, he could be wrong. I still don't think that was a woman."

"But the police artist ..." Sarah started.

"He drew a face on the person, and our source said she wore a veil. The police artist could be wrong. So Suspect #1 is Unidentified Bathroom Person?"

"Now, who else do we have?"

"The gang in Hamilton who may or may not be connected to our stolen quilts."

"Suspect #2—The Hamilton Gang," Sophie wrote.

"Who else do we have?" Sarah asked.

"Well, we have Lonnie, I guess. Just because I believe in him shouldn't automatically eliminate him. I guess we have to consider him," Charles admitted.

"Lonnie is #3," Sophie said as she wrote.

"And the disappearing frame hanger from Hamilton," Sarah shouted. "We can't forget him even though the police have."

"I think he's the most likely suspect," Andy said, and Charles agreed.

"So, he's #4," Sophie said as she wrote another card and tossed it on the pile. "What else do we have?"

The group was silent.

"Is that it?" Sophie asked.

"I think so," Sarah responded.

"Well, we can't solve the crime with this little bit of information. What do we do?" she asked, looking toward Charles. "You're the expert here. What do we do?"

"We locate at least one more quilt, and that will give us our first clue as to what happened."

"Let's get on our computers and search until we find one quilt," Andy responded.

"And I'm going to call Hamilton PD," Charles said, "and see if they have a lead on the guy that sold Tessa the seven quilts. If he didn't steal them himself, he got them from the people who did. That's another lead."

"And I suspect the disappearing quilt framer guy. I wonder if we could get a picture of him and show it to Tessa," Andy speculated.

"I took pictures while they were hanging the quilts," Sarah said. "Let's take a look."

All four friends hurried back to the Parkers' house and went through the photos. "I think we have pictures of four different guys," Charles said. "Was that the whole team?"

"Yes, four," Sarah confirmed.

"Okay. We need to show these pictures to Tessa."

"Should we drive to Hamilton now?" Sarah asked. "Oh, wait. The shop is closed."

"No, my dear. We don't need to do anything so archaic. I'll text them to her right now. Do you have her cell phone number?"

Within moments, the phone rang, and they had their answer back from Tessa. "No, it wasn't any of these men," Tessa said. "I would have recognized him immediately if it had been one of them. I was there while they were assembling the frames."

The group sighed in unison, and Charles opened a beer while Sophie poured wine for the women. "Here, Andy. I bought you a six-pack of sodas. Help yourself."

"Could we make that coffee?" Andy asked. "My meetings have me hooked on drinking coffee at night. Those guys can really put away the coffee!"

Charles turned the television on, and Sarah brought in a bowl of chips and a hot salsa-cheese dip. The four sat without speaking for a few minutes as they enjoyed the refreshments.

"You don't suppose Tessa is involved, do you?" Sophie said, breaking the silence.

"Tessa?" Charles repeated, surprised that Sophie would consider her.

"Who's Tessa?" Andy asked.

Sarah reminded him about the shop in Hamilton with the seven quilts that had been recovered but were being held by the Hamilton police.

"Charles? What do you think?" Sarah asked.

"I was going on your endorsement of her. You both seemed to think she was a victim in the scenario at her shop."

"Well, I think I still do. But …"

"I'm putting her on the list," Sophie announced as she reached for the file box and added a fifth card.

"So, what does that mean?" Andy asked.

"I guess it means that I'll talk to Hal and see what he can find out from Hamilton PD. I'll have him ask if they think she's involved."

Another sigh.

"This dip has put me in the mood for Mexican," Charles suddenly announced as he popped out of his chair. "Let's head over to that new Mexican restaurant, and Sophie, you leave those cards here. We aren't talking about this case for the next two hours."

Chapter 25

"I don't like it that we're even thinking about Tessa," Sophie said as they were working on their wall hangings. "It's hard to picture her, or any quilter for that matter, doing something like this."

"Me too, Sophie, but it was pretty convenient that she ended up with so many of the quilts."

"But, Sarah, she didn't act guilty. Remember how she was when she thought she was in possession of stolen merchandise?"

"How do you think she would act if she had been caught with merchandise she knew was stolen? Probably about the same way is my guess."

"Oh, Sarah, you're beginning to suspect her, aren't you?"

"Sophie, I don't know any more than you do. Surely the police will sort this all out long before we can. Charles took our list of suspects to Hal this morning, and we'll see what he has to say."

"Is Hal even interested anymore? Don't they stop looking once they arrest someone?"

"Oh, I forgot to tell you. They didn't arrest him. The DA said they didn't have enough evidence."

"Well, sure," Sophie said, confirming the DA's opinion. "It's all circumstantial."

"Watching *Law & Order* again, are you?"

"No, reading Michael Connelly."

"Well, either way, you are right, and so was Charles, but that doesn't mean Lonnie is innocent," Sarah responded.

"You don't like him much, do you?" Sophie asked.

"It's not that, Sophie. But remember when Charles was being held for the murder of the foreman? Lonnie's brother just kept right on working on our house and was all sympathetic toward me when I would go talk to him, and all the time he knew he did it. I don't know how Charles was able to forgive him."

"But that wasn't Lonnie."

"I know. I'm being irrational," Sarah responded. "I'll try to be more open-minded about Lonnie, but if it turns out that he did it, I won't be one bit surprised."

"Is that your phone ringing?"

"Oh, you're right. It's hard to hear the landline when we're back here. I'll try to catch it before the machine picks up," she called over her shoulder as she hurried up the hall.

"Hello, Ms. Parker. This is Josie Braxton calling from Amarillo, Texas. You don't know me, but I just got this month's issue of my quilting magazine and was looking at your article about the quilts stolen from your quilt show. What a dreadful thing to happen!"

"Yes, it was heartbreaking for everyone involved," Sarah responded with an inaudible sigh of disappointment. She had received numerous condolence calls over the past weeks from quilters all over the country. She appreciated their concern but had been hoping that the article would create at least one lead.

"I hate to waste your time since I'm not sure about this, but I think I saw some of these quilts at the antique show over at the fairgrounds last week."

Sarah immediately perked up. "Tell me about it."

"Now, I'm not sure they were yours, but when I saw the pictures today, I said to myself, 'Josie, you should call this lady and …' "

"Please, Ms. Braxton, tell me about the quilts," Sarah interrupted, trying to keep the impatience out of her voice.

"Well, I was thumbing through the quilts and even talked briefly to the man who was selling them. I appreciated being able to handle the quilts, but I told him he shouldn't be allowing people to just rummage through them. I started to explain the reason, and he cut me off. He obviously didn't care about the quilts one iota. Anyway, I'm getting off on a tangent. Fred tells me I'm always doing that. I just wanted to let you know that I think at least a few might be with this guy."

"You can't imagine how wonderful this is to hear, Ms. Braxton. …"

"Call me Josie. Folks down here in Amarillo aren't that formal."

"And I'm Sarah. This is the first promising lead we've had. Can you tell me more about this man?"

"Not much, but I did get his card. I was looking at this Asian hand-carved wood table lamp that would be perfect for my living room. We have this … oh, and there I go again. All I meant to say is that he gave me his card since I was interested, but I told him I'd have to talk to my husband. It was way too expensive, but ..."

"Could you please read the card to me so I can write down his contact information?" Sarah said, sorry to again be interrupting, but eager to follow this possible lead.

"Just a minute. I'll get it," the woman responded.

A few moments later, she returned to the phone, and with a deep sigh, she said, "Oh, it only has a website. Do you want that?"

"Definitely." *Anything would be more than what we have now*, Sarah thought.

Josie Braxton read off the website address one letter at a time and then said, "I hope you can get your quilts back, Sarah. Take down my number in case you think of anything I can do to help."

"I appreciate this, Josie," Sarah said as she wrote the number down. "By the way, is the antique show still at the fairgrounds?"

"No, but I think they'll be back next year. I think I'll stick this business card in the mail to you. There's a logo and a few words that might mean something."

"Excellent idea, Josie, and we thank you very much." She gave the woman her address and promised to let her know if the information led them to any of their quilts.

Too late, Sarah said, but only to herself. She thanked the woman profusely and again promised to let her know if they found the quilts.

"I doubt that this will be of much help," Sarah said as she told Charles about the call and handed him the website address.

"Oh, on the contrary," he responded. "There's much I can do with a URL. Let's go to the computer and see what he wants us to see, and then I'll put on my cop hat and look for what he doesn't want us to see."

It was a simple website advertising antiques and collectibles of all types. There were pictures of figurines, furniture, glassware, jewelry, and even clothing that appeared to be from the nineteenth century. Nothing had an exact age, only approximations. There were no quilts, although there was a note that antique embroidery work and quilts were available and would be on display at his next show. The vendor listed his upcoming appearances, which were mostly in the Lower Midwest. The next show was scheduled for mid-December in Phoenix. The exact date and location were not included on the website.

Sarah groaned with disappointment.

"Now, don't get discouraged. There are things I can do to get more information on the owner of this website. Just hang on for an hour or two before you get discouraged."

Two hours passed before Charles appeared in the kitchen where Sarah was turning the roast that she was in the process of browning. "You can get somewhat discouraged now," he announced, looking defeated.

"What happened?"

"He must have been able to track my activities on his website. He shut it down."

"Oh no," Sarah responded, distressed. "What does that mean?"

"Well, there are still things I can do, but they will take longer. If we don't get anywhere with this, you and I might be visiting Phoenix."

"That's not so bad," Sarah responded, looking encouraged. "It's a relatively short flight, I'm sure. When is the next show?"

"Mid-December, I think," Charles replied. "I'm not sure how I'll find out now that the website is gone."

"You can contact Phoenix PD. They'll know."

"Of course," Charles responded, shaking his head. "I can get so one-tracked," he admonished himself as he headed back to his computer room, but he stopped abruptly and returned to the kitchen.

"That's practically Christmas, Sarah. You don't want to be away for Christmas, do you?"

"Find out exactly when it is before we panic, Charles. If it's mid-December, that's not bad. It would be a great Christmas present for our friends if we found the quilts that quickly."

"Don't you have Christmas gifts to complete?"

"Sophie and I are almost finished. Jason and Jenny have invited the whole family to their house for Christmas dinner, so we'll just celebrate Christmas then. We can make this work, Charles. Just find out when it is."

Chapter 26

"I'm going, too," Sophie announced, holding her chin high with a look of absolute determination. "You need me to help identify the quilts, and besides, I've never been to Phoenix. I understand they have year-round sunshine and excellent desert resorts."

"We won't be there long enough to enjoy a resort, Sophie. It's too close to Christmas, but Charles will find us a nice hotel."

"Sure," Charles agreed as he walked into the room, catching the end of the conversation. "Do you think Norman will want to go?"

"I'll ask him," Sophie responded.

"Bad news," Sophie reported a few minutes later after a quick call to Norman. "He's already committed to Christmas at the cabin with the kids, and they plan to go to the cabin ahead of time. He said it's too much of a crunch for him, so count me out too."

"You're going to the cabin for Christmas?" Sarah asked, looking surprised. "I thought you were going to be with us at Jason's. Otherwise, you'll miss being with your son and granddaughter."

"No, I'm not going to the cabin. He invited me, but I don't want to be with his family and miss being with my own. So I could go to Phoenix, but I don't want to intrude on you and Charles."

"Rubbish!" Charles called out from the den.

"Excuse me?" Sophie replied, indignantly. "Was that meant for me?"

"Yes, it was. You are welcome to come with us. Besides, I need you and your card file. There's no telling what we'll find there!"

Sophie turned to her friend and whispered, "I just love that man!"

Two weeks later, Norman drove the Parkers and Sophie to the airport. "I'll miss you, sweetie," he whispered in Sophie's ear as they parted just before reaching the security gates.

"You can't go any farther without a ticket, sir," a man in uniform announced. Norman quickly kissed Sophie on the cheek. They were both beginning to tear up but laughed at themselves.

"I'll only be gone a few days," Sophie assured him.

"I know, sweetie, but I'll be leaving the day after you return. I'm going to miss you," he added as he backed away, still waving.

As the three approached the security booth, Sophie saw people removing their shoes and putting them into a tray. "Why are they doing that?" she asked.

"Security measures," Charles replied offhandedly.

"And you don't mind?"

"I don't mind. I'm trusting these folks to keep us safe," Charles responded.

"Well, you aren't as old as I am, and you don't realize how hard it is to reach down and untie shoes. Then I have to get them off without sitting down and without toppling over on my head!"

Sophie's voice was escalating, and the other passengers were beginning to crowd around to see what the commotion was about. Fortunately, Charles was able to use his past law-enforcement experience to move them away gently.

As Sophie approached the guard, she announced her objections in a loud and demanding voice.

"We're going to get thrown off the plane," Charles whispered to Sarah. Then he attempted to calm Sophie down, but she was on a roll and dismissed him.

"But miss," the man kept saying in an attempt to respond to her complaints.

"Sophie," Charles finally said in a compelling voice that finally got her attention. "Listen to the man. He's trying to tell you something."

"What?" she demanded sharply.

"Elderly people don't have to remove their shoes. Walk on through."

"What?" she responded in dismay. "You discriminate against elderly people? I'll certainly take my shoes off if I want to." Moments later, both of Sophie's shoes were in the basket and rolling toward the x-ray machine. "I guess I told them," she muttered.

"It's going to be a long trip," Charles whispered to his wife as they were heading for the gate.

* * * * *

"This isn't what I expected at all," Sophie exclaimed, looking around at the palm trees that lined the drive up to the hotel entrance. "Oh, is that the hotel? It looks like a mansion, and I sure didn't expect all those palm trees."

"What did you expect, Sophie?" Sarah asked as they pulled up to the front entrance of the hotel. Two men hurried to their rental car and unloaded their luggage. The porter accompanied them to the clerk's desk, and the valet whisked the car away.

"Well, I guess I pictured miles of sand and maybe a mirage or two. Maybe cactus and lizards, but I was hoping I wouldn't have to go near them."

"And what did you picture yourself doing out in that godforsaken desert?"

"Hmm. I guess I didn't get that far in my thinking. But this is incredible. Oh, Charles," she said as they stepped into the lobby. She covered her mouth with her one free hand and muttered, "What have I gotten myself into? This looks very expensive."

Charles laughed and reached for the bag she was pushing. "I have this covered, and I got a great deal, so don't give it another thought."

"Oh, but I want to pay for my own room."

"Actually, I got us a suite, and the couch opens into a king-size bed. I'm going to sleep there, and you girls will get the bedroom."

"Oh, I can't impose like that. . . ."

"Not another word," Sarah interrupted her friend. "It's settled. Besides, we're going to be out most of the time."

"What will we be doing?" Sophie asked as they followed the porter to their room.

"Tomorrow morning, we're signed up for a bus tour of the sights. I like to do that just to get oriented whenever I'm traveling," Sarah said. "We'll ride through the city and stop at a few shops and galleries. We'll see Camelback Mountain from a distance, and later we'll drive outside the city, where you'll be able to see the desert you were expecting to see."

By this time, they had arrived at their room. Sophie noted that the bedroom had two king-size beds. "Charles, I don't see why you want to sleep in the living room. Why can't we all sleep here?"

"I thought you girls would want your privacy," Charles responded.

"Poppycock!" Sophie exclaimed. "When we went on the cruise, we hung out together in our pajamas all the time. You and Sarah take that bed. I want the one by the bathroom."

"Okay by me," Charles responded. "As Sarah said, I doubt we'll be spending much time up here anyway. What else do we have on our agenda?" he asked, slipping his arm around his wife.

"I think we should go to the Heard Museum tomorrow afternoon. We'll be sitting on the bus all morning and ready for a stroll, and I think Sophie and I will enjoy the displays of their handwoven blankets, serapes, and other textiles. The Southwestern colors are extraordinary, and we might get ideas for a quilt—maybe something Southwestern to remember the trip."

"Oh, look!" Sophie squealed. "Here are brochures, and this one is for the Heard Museum gift shop. Just look at the silver jewelry! I'm going home with a silver necklace around my neck. Look at this one. It's a squash blossom necklace made with silver and turquoise. It was made by the Navajo. This is the one I'm wearing home!"

"Did you see the price on that one?" Sarah asked.

"No. Hand me my glasses." There was a long silence while Sophie digested the price before saying, "Well, I think this is too massive for my short frame. Maybe I'll look for something in beads."

While Sophie was in the bathroom arranging her toiletries, Charles took the brochure to Sarah and pointed out the squash blossom necklace that Sophie had admired. $25,000. They both chuckled, and Sarah said, "I agree it's too massive for her short frame."

"So, that takes care of our first full day here," Charles announced when Sophie returned to the room. "The next day is the beginning of the antique show, and I think we should get there early. We don't know exactly what we're looking for," Charles said.

"Quilts. That's what we're looking for. Quilts," Sophie announced.

"Yes, but what if we find that everyone has quilts. We don't know which vendor is the one Josie told us about."

"So we just look around," Sophie responded with a shrug. "Maybe we should go early."

Charles sighed and shook his head. "Yes, good idea."

They decided to order room service the first evening since all three of them were worn out from the trip.

Their first full day in Phoenix was spent sightseeing as planned and ended with the three friends being even more exhausted than the night before, but they decided to have a light dinner in the hotel's café. They had sampled the food at every stop along their sightseeing tour.

Chapter 27

Early the next morning, Sarah ordered breakfast while Sophie showered, and Charles went down to the gym. By opening time, the three friends were standing at the entrance to the fairgrounds waiting to purchase their tickets. Sophie was wearing her new, brightly colored beads.

"Have you talked to Norman this morning?" Sarah asked.

"Yes, I called him from the balcony before you two woke up."

"Did you ask how things are going with Barney?"

"He and Barney are doing just fine. Norman decided to take you up on your offer for him to stay at your house. He was worried about Barney being alone if he just dropped by every few hours. He seems to be enjoying having the animals around. I think he misses having a dog."

"That high-end building of his doesn't allow pets?" Sarah responded with surprise.

"Oh, they allow them. He just wants to wait until he's fully retired and living in his cabin in Kentucky."

This was the first Sarah had heard about any plans for moving. She wondered if Sophie would be going with him. Her heart ached at the thought of her friend moving away, but she was beginning to see that it was inevitable. Her friend was in love, and Norman was a good man. Sarah smiled to think of her friend finding the happiness she had with Charles.

"Where shall we start?" Sophie asked, interrupting Sarah's thoughts.

"Let's go to the far right-hand side of the arena and do each aisle in order. Are you going to be okay with this much walking, Sophie?"

"No problem. Besides, I saw carts by the entrance. You can get me one if I can't make it."

The first two aisles displayed home furnishings from the eighteenth and nineteenth centuries but at outlandish prices, according to Sophie. "Who would pay these prices?"

Sarah occasionally asked a vendor if they carried antique quilts, but was consistently told no. One vendor directed them to a large display in aisle four, which featured rugs and fabric items. They passed by the china displays without slowing down, but when they arrived at the fourth aisle, they moved more slowly.

"Do you have quilts?" Sarah asked sweetly.

"I sure do, but you folks got here early. I've hardly started unpacking the cloth." The man disappeared behind a divider and returned with a pile of crocheted and embroidered table cloths and napkins. "If any of this stuff appeals to you, just dig into the pile," the man said as he disappeared behind the divider again.

When he returned, he had dresses from the 1800s. He placed them on a rack he must have had specially made for them. "They're so small," Sophie commented. "Were people really that small back then?"

"They must have been. Charles and I went to a church built in 1820, and the seats were so narrow we hardly fit."

"Don't know why that is," the man said, obviously listening in. "Probably nutrition or medicine. Try on one of those women's hats over there. I'll bet they're way too small. That's just the way it was," he added as he headed back behind the divider.

He returned with a tall stack of quilts. "This what you gals are lookin' for?" he asked.

"Exactly," Sarah responded excitedly, but then had second thoughts about displaying her excitement. "I'm decorating my whole house with items from the nineteenth century, and I need quilts for all the beds. Do you mind if I pick through this pile?"

"Not at all. That's what they're here for."

Sarah poked Sophie and whispered that she should remain calm and make no accusations if they found one of their quilts. "Just wait for Charles to come."

"Where is he anyway?" Sophie asked as she moved the first four quilts to the side, where she had started a rejection pile.

"He decided to scope out the whole fair to save us time. He'll be back with a list of vendors with quilts."

"So you're looking for lots of quilts?" the man asked, obviously overhearing their last comment.

"Perhaps ten or so, I think," Sarah responded coolly. She wondered how she could lie so easily. *Maybe because I'm talking to a potential criminal*, she thought. *It's okay to lie to a criminal.* She remembered someone saying that on a crime show.

By this time, they had most of the quilts moved to the rejection pile. "They don't even come close," Sophie said, having surreptitiously checked the pictures on her cell phone.

"These aren't quite what I'm looking for. Do you have any others?"

"Sorry, miss. That's it. There's not much money in quilts, so I don't often carry but a few. I haven't sold one in the past year. I might just give up on quilts."

Sarah thanked the man for his time, and she and Sophie moved on. At the end of the aisle, they ran into Charles, who had a broad smile on his face. "I found our guy," he announced proudly.

"And? Does he have the quilts? Wait. How do you know he's our guy?"

"Breathe, Sarah," he replied to his overexcited wife. "I didn't ask about quilts. That's for you and Sophie to do. I just saw his pile of cards and picked up one and casually stuck it in my pocket." He pulled the card out and handed it to Sarah. "Have you ever seen that card before?"

"It's our guy," she exclaimed, immediately recognizing the card color and style.

"Same card, same website," Charles pointed out. "Not sure what that means, but get your 3″ by 5″ cards ready, Sophie. We have ourselves a thief."

But before approaching the vendor, the three sat down at a picnic table in the food vendors' area and discussed strategy. Charles was emphatic about not making any accusations or displaying any telling responses when they saw one of their quilts. "I will quietly call the police from my cell phone," he said. "There are two officers standing by."

"How did that happen?" Sarah asked.

"Hal set it up, and the officers are waiting for my call."

Sophie looked at Sarah. "I'm a little nervous, but I guess we're safe. Don't you think, Sarah?"

"We're safe. We have Charles, and he has backup. We're fine."

"Okay, then, this is it," Charles responded.

"Ready, captain," Sophie announced with a quick salute.

"Remember, Sophie. No matter what you see, or how excited you get, don't let on," Sarah whispered.

"You already told me that," Sophie grumbled.

"Good morning, ladies. What can I do for you today?" The man at the booth appeared friendly and had a compelling smile as he greeted Sarah and Sophie. Charles was stationed at the end of the aisle, where he pretended to be carefully examining a harp-back side chair when, in fact, he hadn't taken his eyes off the two women.

"I came here hoping to find a few quilts for my new home, but I'm not having much luck. Are these the only ones you have?" she asked with a dismissive gesture toward the few quilts folded on the table. She and Sophie had already looked at them, and they were not from Middletown.

"Oh no, I have several dozen," the man assured them. "I'll run out to my van and get them." Calling across the aisle, he said, "Larry, can you keep an eye on my booth? I need to run out to the van."

"Sure," the man named Larry responded.

"I'll be right back," he vendor said, turning to Sarah and Sophie. "I usually don't get many calls for quilts, so I just put out a few until I get a request. It will just take a minute," he added as he headed for the side door. A few minutes later, he returned with an armload of quilts and began spreading them out on the counter. "Now, these are probably what you're looking for," he said. "They're in mint condition."

Curious to know what the man would charge for "mint condition," Sarah turned the tag over and read $1,800.

"Oh my," she responded.

"Everything in my booth is negotiable," the man added quickly. "But look at the quilting. See how close those stitches are, and the pattern of the quilting adds to the worth of the quilt, as you probably know. This is a very intricate pattern. Now, if you don't want to go that high, take a look at these, but I have to tell you, there are flaws. See this binding?"

"It's badly frayed," Sarah remarked. "How about that one over there?"

While Sarah kept the man occupied, Sophie was going through all the quilts and occasionally glancing at her cell phone. When Sarah saw the vendor notice her looking at the cell phone, she said, "Hasn't Laura called yet, Sophie? I wonder where she is. She was supposed to meet us at the gate."

For a fleeting moment, Sophie looked confused, but she quickly caught on. "Well, if she's standing there waiting, she can just wait. I told her to call my cell." The man lost interest in the conversation and pulled a few more quilts to the top of the pile.

"You might like one of these. They are in the $500 to $700 range. No flaws to speak of, but the quilting is simpler."

"These look like they might be Amish," Sophie said to Sarah.

"They are," the man confirmed. "You have a good eye. I bought those last spring when I was up in Lancaster. Excellent work. Now the Amish tend to use solid colors with a good bit of black, as you can see. But just look at those tiny stitches."

Turning away from the table, Sarah said, "Let me see if Laura called on my phone. I'm getting worried about her," and she quickly scanned through her pictures of Ruth's Amish quilts.

"Is this all you have?" she ultimately asked the man after examining every quilt in detail.

"I'm afraid so," he responded. "Do you mind if I help that man? He's been waiting for quite a while. If you need me, just holler."

"Of course," Sarah said, suddenly realizing a few customers had joined them at the booth. "Just let me and my friend take one more look at these. Surely we can find a couple that will be right for my home."

Relieved to be out from under the vendor's close scrutiny, Sarah and Sophie went through the dozens of quilts that were now spread out on the counter. "Not one," Sophie whispered.

"I know. I was so sure we'd find at least one."

Charles saw that the two women had stopped digging through the pile of quilts and had stepped back from the counter. He decided to join them and see if he could help. "No luck?" he said as he walked up.

"I'm afraid not, Charles." Noticing that the vendor was now listening to their conversation, she added, "I had something very specific in mind, and I guess I'll never find it."

"What exactly did you have in mind?" the vendor asked.

Sarah mentioned the Civil War fabrics in Andy's quilt and added, "and maybe something with browns."

"Sure wish I could help you, but this is it. I've emptied the van. Why don't you look around? There are several other vendors carrying quilts, and if you don't find anything, come back here. I'll give you 30% off on any quilt you choose from here."

"Just on one?" Sophie asked.

"Maybe more," the man said, laughing. "We'll see."

"You can't beat that deal," Charles exclaimed. "Come on, ladies, let's get something to eat before we do any more shopping."

Turning to the quilt vendor, he said, "Thanks for your patience with my gals. We'll probably be back."

"I hope so," the man said cheerfully, turning to the couple who had been waiting. "Sorry to keep you folks waiting," he said. "How can I help you?"

* * * * *

"She'll be a while," Charles remarked as he and Sophie found an empty table. It was approaching noon, and there were long lines at the food vendors' booths. Sarah had insisted on waiting in the line for hot dogs and sodas.

"Here she comes carrying a tray," Sophie exclaimed. "That didn't take long."

"This nice-looking cowboy let me cut in line," Sarah announced. Charles frowned and scanned the line, looking to see who may have been flirting with his wife.

"He was young enough to be my grandson, Charles. Relax!"

Charles picked up his hot dog but glanced up at the line a couple of times just to make sure. After a while, he relaxed and asked, "So, about the quilts. Did you see anything familiar?"

"We sure did. We saw five quilts that were the same patterns as ours," Sarah responded. "There were lots of star patterns, several crazy quilts, and a Robbing Peter to Pay Paul, but none of them were ours."

"Are you sure?" Charles asked.

"Absolutely, Charles. I have the pictures right there. The colors were wrong. The sizes were wrong. Even the quilting was wrong. They weren't our quilts."

"But what about the woman in Amarillo? She said she saw our quilts," Sophie asked.

"I think Josie's intentions were good," Sarah responded. "She was looking at the magazine article and recalling the quilts she had seen in the show. They were the right patterns but the wrong colors. This man doesn't have our quilts and probably never did."

"Then why did he shut down his website when you were on it?" Sophie asked Charles as she reached for her second hot dog.

"I checked today, and it's up again, and it's still on his card. I think that might have been more of a simple coincidence. He probably shut it down temporarily to update it after the Amarillo show," Charles replied, "and that just happened to be when I was trying to access it."

"You mean we wasted our time coming here?" Sophie asked.

"No, I had a great time. Didn't you?" Sarah asked. "I'm glad we came."

"Actually, yes, I did," Sophie responded, "and I still am. In fact, I'd like to go back and look at his quilts again.

There was this small one there I really liked, and I think it would look sensational on my bedroom wall. Would you hang it for me if I buy it, Charles? Norman isn't very handy that way."

"I would be happy to do that, Sophie," Charles responded.

After walking through most of the other aisles and seeing no other quilts, the group returned to the previous quilt vendor, and Sophie purchased the small Turkey red and white Broken Star quilt, taking advantage of his 30% off offer. Sarah considered buying one so she would have a change for her vintage guest room but decided to make one using reproduction fabrics instead.

"What a deal," Sophie exclaimed, hugging her purchase, as they headed for their rental car.

The next morning they returned home without incident. Sophie left her shoes on and walked through the security check peacefully and carried her purchase onto the plane as her carry-on. Charles had checked all their baggage.

As the plane was descending, Sarah took her husband's hand and said, "I wish we were bringing good news to our friends."

"I'm glad you didn't tell the women in the quilt club where we were going. At least we didn't raise their hopes."

They weren't aware of one person who knew they were going to Phoenix and was delighted to see them heading off in the wrong direction.

Chapter 28

It was early Christmas morning, and Charles and Sarah decided to have a pancake breakfast. They had exchanged their gifts the evening before, a tradition they had started the first year they were together. It freed them up to spend Christmas Day with family.

They arrived at Sarah's son's house at noon and were immediately joined by Sophie and her son, Tim, with his wife, Martha, and Tim's daughter, Penny. Jennifer's parents had flown in the day before and were staying with Jason, Jennifer, and their two children: Alaina, who was now five, and Jonathan, soon to turn three.

The children immediately began ripping the paper off the presents their friends and relatives had brought for them and were running around excitedly showing them to everyone. Jennifer tried to keep up with the wrapping paper, which was being strewn around the room, but threw her hands up at one point and said, "Ah, it's only paper." She headed for the kitchen.

Sarah was surprised her son was comfortable with all the chaos. When he was growing up, they had opened one gift at a time in a more orderly manner, but Sarah was not one to interfere and decided to simply relax and enjoy the children's excitement. It wasn't long before Alaina and Jonathan had both settled down with their favorite gifts.

Sophie and Sarah joined Jennifer in the kitchen and helped the young mother serve the magnificent dinner she had prepared. "How did you manage to do all this with the children and a houseful of guests?" Sarah asked.

"You can do anything on Christmas," Jennifer responded with a broad smile. "It's a magical day! I love Christmas, with the decorations and the music and especially having the family all together."

Jennifer was her son's second wife and, watching her today, Sarah knew Jason had made the right decision when he married her. Jason and his first wife, Joyce, had lost their son when he was eleven, and it was a tragedy their marriage couldn't survive. *He would be twenty now*, Sarah thought, and Charles saw a shadow of sadness cross her face.

"Are you okay?" he asked.

"I am," she responded with a smile. "Let's find our seats at the table. Jenny's about to bring the turkey out."

"I'm so glad my son married your daughter," Sophie whispered to Sarah during dinner. "It means we'll all be together for holidays forever. I love this!"

"I am too, Sophie. I'm sorry Charles couldn't be with his sons and grandsons today, but we're planning a trip to Colorado in the spring to see them."

"I know he misses his boys, but he's with family right now, and he looks happy," Sophie said.

"He does, doesn't he?" Sarah responded with love in her eyes as she watched her husband lifting little Jonathan into his booster chair.

A light snow had been falling since the previous evening, and by midafternoon the children were eager to make a snowman. Charles and Timothy took the two kids outside while the rest of the family watched from the living room window. Tim lay down in the snow and taught Alaina how to make a snow angel while Charles taught Jonathan how to roll a snowball in the snow to make it grow bigger and bigger—a process that fascinated the young boy.

Once there was the semblance of a snowman, Sarah slipped on her coat and took a carrot out for its nose and one of Jason's baseball caps to finish it off.

"Why can't we bring it in the house?" Jonathan pleaded.

Charles attempted to explain the concept of melting, but he stopped when the boy's lip began to quiver. "Jason," Charles called out. "Your son needs you."

"That's the joy of grandparenting," he whispered to Sarah on their way in. "You can give them back to their parents when the going gets tough."

* * * * *

"It was a perfect day," Charles commented as he pulled into their garage. They could hear Barney's urgent bark as they approached the kitchen door. "Sounds like Barney has a problem," he added as he unlocked the door between the garage and the kitchen.

Once they were inside, Barney stopped only long enough to bump Sarah's leg with his nose before running to the backyard door and scratching eagerly to get out.

"Desperate, are you?" Sarah commented, but when she opened the door, she realized he wasn't heading for his usual corner, but instead was slowly creeping toward a hissing black and white creature in the middle of the yard that resembled a Halloween ornament. The creature seemed to be standing on its tiptoes, with its back arched high in the air and its hair puffed out like a porcupine. The closer Barney got to it, the more ferociously it hissed.

Sarah, concerned for Barney's safety, started to call him back, but Charles laid his hand on her arm and said with a smile, "It's okay. He knows what he's doing." Charles had already figured out what it was.

Barney continued to move slowly toward the creature, but now his head was close to the ground as he sniffed for a clue. While hissing and growling at the approaching dog, the small creature stood its ground until Barney was actually nose to nose with it.

It hissed and took a swipe at Barney's nose. Barney yelped and backed up a couple of steps.

"It's a cat!" Sarah exclaimed. By this time, she and Charles were outside, but they stayed near the door, not wanting to upset the delicate balance and cause one or both of the animals to suffer an injury.

"A very self-confident cat," Charles remarked, "judging from the way it's taking on Barney."

The two animals remained almost nose to nose, but slowly the cat's back began to relax into a normal position, and Sarah could see now that it was a kitten and not nearly as big as it had attempted to make itself look.

Barney finally broke the tension by straightening up, shaking the snow off his fur, and walking over to his private corner of the yard where he could do his business partially hidden by the shed.

The cat watched him intently until Sarah moved and the cat's head whipped around to check out Sarah and Charles.

"Meow," it called out in a soft, compelling voice.

"Are you okay, little one?" Sarah asked as she approached the cat, hoping not to scare it off.

"Oh, this is a young kitten," she exclaimed as she got closer. "Probably only five or six months old."

"You're a brave little one," she cooed as she reached down to see if the kitten would allow her to pick it up. But instead of resisting, the kitten melted in her arms and began purring.

"The cat is freezing," she said, tucking it under the front of her coat. "Let's take it inside and see if there's any identification. We can call the owner."

Sarah sat at the kitchen table with the kitten on her lap as they searched for a collar.

"It's a boy," Charles announced, "but I don't think there's a collar." The kitten's fur was so long and thick they couldn't immediately tell whether or not there was a collar hidden under all the fluff.

"Such a pretty little boy," Sarah said as she sat him up on the table where Charles had spread a towel. "Look at that face!" He was primarily black with snow-white fur around his mouth, down his chest, and across his underbelly. "That's called a tuxedo cat," Sarah told her husband, who had never had pets before marrying her.

"He has white feet like Boots," Charles noted, "and will you look at those ears!" The kitten's ears were large and pointed, with little wisps of black hair sticking straight up on the tips.

"Such an endearing little fur ball," Sarah cooed, and the kitten purred even louder.

"*Meow!*" This cry was much louder and more demanding and didn't come from the kitten. Charles and Sarah looked up simultaneously to see their Boots on top of the kitchen cabinets, looking down with both annoyance and disdain.

"It's okay, Bootsy," Sarah said, reverting to the cat's previous name when she was a baby. Barney had discovered Boots when the little kitten was a few weeks old and abandoned in the park during a snowstorm. She had become part of their family, although she chose to live on top of the kitchen cabinets. Sarah insisted that she come down for her meals; however, when Sarah wasn't paying attention, Charles would sometimes slip her food bowl to her on top of the refrigerator. When he did, she would always purr loudly while she ate.

Boots abruptly turned her back on the activity in the kitchen and curled up in the furry bed Sarah had placed on top of the cabinet in the far corner where she preferred to sleep. Clearly, she intended to ignore the intrusion.

There was a scratching at the back door, and Sarah jumped. "Oh no! We left Barney outside."

Charles opened the door, and Barney burst into the room and immediately located the kitten. He stood next to Sarah's chair and stretched up to see what was happening on the table. There was the kitten, looking totally at home sitting in the middle of the kitchen table eating Boots' food. Barney looked questioningly at Sarah.

"This is just temporary, Barney. We'll find his family tomorrow."

Chapter 29

"Charles, is Barney on your side of the bed?" Sarah was just waking up and noticed that Barney's bed was empty.

"He's not on this side, but he might have moved to his bed in the kitchen since he was irritated with us last night for bringing the kitten into the house."

"Oh, the kitten," she exclaimed, still not awake enough to focus on their Christmas night experience. Charles had found a small box in the garage, and Sarah had filled it with fabric scraps to make a soft bed for the kitten.

"Where did you end up putting his box?" Charles asked. Barney had objected to it being in the master bedroom or the kitchen.

"I put it in the guest bathroom," she replied as she slipped on her robe and slippers and went down the hallway. Moments later, she exclaimed, "He's not here. The box is empty."

"I'm on my way," Charles responded.

Together they searched Charles' den and Sarah's sewing room, checking behind and under the furniture. From there, they went through the living room and dining room but without finding him.

As they stepped into the kitchen, they both spotted the tender sight at the same moment. Sarah touched Charles' arm to keep him from disturbing them. "Just look at that," she said softly.

Barney was asleep on his side. Sarah could hear his gentle snore. He had the kitten tucked up under his arm and against his warm chest. Sarah thought she could hear a soft purring sound. "He's listening to Barncy's heartbeat," she whispered to her husband.

Once Barney was aware of their presence, he crawled out of bed and turned to look at the kitten, who was now lying on his back and stretching. Noticing Barney, he mewed softly.

"Come on, Barney," Charles said, leading the dog to the back door. The dog was reluctant to leave the kitten, but Charles assured him it would be okay. After he let Barney out, he went to the garage to find another box and filled it with Boots' litter. The kitten knew exactly what it was for.

After feeding all the animals, Charles and Sarah sat down to a simple breakfast of oatmeal with raisins. "We need to make a sign and post it on the telephone poles," Sarah announced.

"We don't have telephone poles in the Village," Charles reminded her.

"True, but he didn't necessarily live in the Village, and there are telephone poles on the streets around us."

"That's true," Charles responded thoughtfully. "And there are bulletin boards in the Community Center and the nursing home, and even out by the front gate."

"When I was young," Sarah reminisced, "there were always signs posted on the telephone poles about lost pets or local activities. I used to love walking to school and reading all the signs. I would daydream about seeing one of the missing animals and returning it to its owner."

"You were a softy even then," he commented affectionately. "But you're right. We need to make a sign and post it around the neighborhood. I'll take his picture and make a sign just as soon as I get home."

"You're going out?"

"Yes, I have a meeting with Hal and two of his officers to discuss the quilt case this morning, but it won't take long."

"Before you leave, there's one other thing. I don't know what to call the kitten, and I think he needs a name. What do you think of ...?"

"Not yet, Sarah," Charles interrupted his wife. "Once we name him, he's got both feet, possibly all four feet, in the door. He belongs to someone."

"But he didn't even have a collar," she replied. "Certainly not someone who cared about him."

"We can't assume that, Sarah. I'll make the signs, and we'll see what happens, okay?"

Sarah sighed but nodded her agreement. "I'll write something up and take the picture while you're gone, and you can make a sign on the computer later."

"Thank you, hon," he responded as he kissed her on the cheek and pulled his heavy coat on. "I think it's going to snow more," he commented as he opened the garage door.

* * * * *

"I'm having second thoughts about Lonnie, Hal. Maybe he was involved in some way."

"He's been my number one suspect throughout the investigation. Why the change of heart?"

"I'm not sure. Maybe because we're running out of other ideas, and it seems like it keeps coming back to Lonnie. He had access. He got rid of the locks, which could have been evidence of what happened. He's been in trouble with the law. Granted, it was many years ago, and it appears that he's been straight for a while, but maybe he hasn't been so straight. Maybe he just hasn't been caught."

"My thoughts exactly, Charlie. I mean Charles."

Charles chuckled. "Don't worry about it, Hal. But getting back to Lonnie Dunkin, I certainly don't think he stole the quilts himself. What would he do with them? He couldn't sell them because we'd be watching. It doesn't make sense for him to be the one who actually took the quilts."

"I agree. I think he facilitated it for someone else," Hal responded.

"But who?"

"Well, maybe the Hamilton gang," the detective responded. "That's what Hamilton PD thinks."

"They think it was Lonnie?" Charles asked with surprise.

"No, they think the gang had a contact here who helped them with access. I'm the one who thinks it was Lonnie Dunkin."

"And now I'm beginning to think so, too," Charles said sadly.

"Glad you're looking at this with an open mind," Hal responded. "Last week, we talked to Jeff Holbrook, the administrator over there, just to get his take on this Dunkin guy."

"And?"

"Holbrook is his boss. He said the guy's okay. He seems to have money problems, and he frequently tries to borrow against his paycheck, but Holbrook says he does his job."

"Maybe Lonnie saw an opportunity for some quick cash," Charles said thoughtfully. "On the other hand," he added quickly, "how could he turn three dozen quilts into quick cash?"

"Thus the connection with the Hamilton gang," the detective said.

"Hmm," Charles groaned. "But it just doesn't feel right to me."

"He's the only person who could leave the door unlocked so someone could get in."

"Maybe Lonnie just accidentally left the auditorium unlocked when he took the mayor's wife home, and someone walked in and took the quilts."

"A crime of convenience? Interesting thought, Charlie, but why would there just happen to be a thief standing by hoping to discover an unlocked door?"

"Okay, that idea doesn't make much sense, does it?" Charles replied. "Why would the thief have been there unless it was prearranged?"

"And that brings us right back to Lonnie Dunkin, if he, in fact, left the door unlocked."

"But the door wasn't necessarily left unlocked, Hal. The thief might have picked the lock or broken it somehow."

"And we'll never know, will we, since Dunkin got rid of the locks," Hal asked rhetorically.

"I don't want to think it was Lonnie," Charles said sadly. "I like the man, but …"

"We'll take another look," Hal responded. "You don't need to follow up on this. I know he's a friend."

"Thanks, Hal. I hope we're wrong."

Chapter 30

When Charles returned home, Sarah handed him a handwritten draft of a sign and her cell phone. "The pictures are there. I took several views. He's so cute."

Charles scrolled to the pictures and laughed. "How did you get him to pose like this?" he asked. The kitten was sitting on the table facing the camera with his beautiful yellow eyes staring right into the lens. His wild silky fur stuck out all over his body. "What an adorable little fellow," Charles murmured as a look of sadness crossed his face.

"You want to keep him, don't you?" Sarah teased.

"I wouldn't object too strongly if it should come to that," he responded.

Two days later, there had still been no response to the posters, and Sarah was getting antsy about naming the kitten. "We can't keep calling him 'the kitten.' "

"Tomorrow," Charles responded, "if we haven't heard from anyone, we'll stop by Barney's vet and make sure he doesn't have a microchip. And if not, maybe we'll think about at least giving him a name. Did you call Animal Rescue today to see if they'd had any calls?"

"I did, and they haven't heard from anyone about a missing cat."

The next day they confirmed that the kitten hadn't been chipped, and the vet took a look at him and said he was in excellent shape. As they were leaving, Sarah said, "See, you wouldn't name him, and now he has a number on his permanent record instead of a name."

"I don't think that will hinder his chances for future success in the cat world," Charles responded. "Anyway, if we end up naming him, we'll ask them to change it on his record."

Sarah smiled, realizing that Charles was beginning to see that the cute little kitten would probably become part of their family.

As they were getting ready for bed, the phone rang. Barney had moved back to his bed in their room and was in his bed with the kitten tucked up under his arm. Charles answered the phone in their bedroom, and Sarah realized he was talking to the owner of the cat. Her heart sank as she looked down at the two curled up in Barney's bed. When Charles walked out of the room, still talking to the caller, she didn't follow him, not wanting to hear the bad news yet.

A few minutes later, he came into the room and put the phone in its cradle. "Well, my dear, it's time to name the kitten."

"What?" she squealed. "Weren't you talking to the owner?"

"Not exactly. I was talking to the son of the owner. His mother had a stroke on Christmas Day, and they think the cat must have run out while the paramedics were there."

"And?"

"And the son said that after her discharge, his mother would be going home with him permanently. His wife is allergic to cats, and he asked if we might know someone who could take him."

"And you said?"

"I said I certainly did know of a very nice lady who was hoping she could keep the little tyke. So if you want to talk about names now ..."

"Look at them," she exclaimed, pointing to the dog bed. "See how he's all tucked under Barney's arm?"

"Yes?" Charles responded, not sure where this was going.

"How about Tucker?"

"Tucker," he repeated. "I like it. We could even call him Tux for short since he's wearing a tuxedo."

"We'll see," she responded with a look that clearly said she wasn't sure about the nickname.

* * * * *

The phone was answered with "Burgess residence."

"How incredibly formal," Sarah responded, and Caitlyn giggled.

"I knew it was you," the young girl said excitedly. "We've had such a great time, Aunt Sarah. I wish you'd been here. Papa and I went shopping when he first got here, and I helped him find gifts for Aunt Maddie. He got her a beautiful bed jacket. I'm not sure it was the right thing to get because she said, 'People still wear these?' when she opened it, but she's had it on every night when I go in to say goodnight."

The girl chattered on about her father's visit and how the two strangers—her father and her aunt Maddie—were spending hours catching up on all the lost years. "Can I tell you a secret, Aunt Sarah?"

"I suppose so," Sarah responded, not really wanting to know something she shouldn't, but still curious.

"Papa has asked Aunt Maddie to come live with us, and she's actually thinking about it!"

"That would be nice, Caitlyn," Sarah responded but wondered whether a move at this point in the woman's life was a good idea. She'd been settled in Omaha for many years and had friends, her church, and her various volunteer activities. Sarah knew that sometimes it was a mistake to uproot an elderly person even if you think it's for their own good. "Just make sure in the end that it's your aunt Maddie's decision and not your father's. It might look like the right thing to do on the surface, but sometimes older people end up very unhappy when they leave everything they know."

"I've heard Aunt Maddie and Papa talking about that very thing. Aunt Maddie said she wants to give it some serious thought, and she wouldn't consider doing it before next summer."

"That will give her plenty of time to think about it," Sarah responded, relieved that they weren't making any rash decisions. "So, what else have you been doing?"

"Mostly eating!" Caitlyn responded with her usual delightful giggle. "I've gained five pounds since Papa came, but we've been eating out, and the food in Omaha is unbelievable. I used to think I'd like to be a vegetarian, but once I tasted these steaks, there's no chance I'll ever do that."

"And I assume your dad is having a good time, too?"

"Here," Caitlyn said. "He wants to talk to you."

"Hi, Sarah. How's everything back home?"

"We miss you," Sarah responded, "but it sounds like you're having a great time."

The two friends talked about the time they each had spent with family and friends. Sarah told Andy about their trip to Phoenix and recounted a few Sophie tales that got him laughing. He particularly enjoyed the shoe episode at the airport.

"What a character that woman is," he responded. "But what would we do without her?"

They talked for a while about the possibility of Maddie coming to live with them, and Sarah suggested they have her come for a visit first.

"Great idea," Andy responded. "Maybe I can get her to come back with me next week just to meet people and see what it's like."

"Am I on speaker?" Sarah asked.

"No, why?"

"I didn't know if you'd mentioned the missing quilts to your aunt, but I wanted to let you know that there's been no news. The detective has been questioning Lonnie Dunkin, but they haven't charged him. And the magazine article has resulted in a few calls, but nothing has panned out so far. I just wanted you to know. We can talk more about it when you come home."

"Caitlyn advised against bringing it up, and I'm glad she did. I wouldn't want anything to cloud this holiday. It's been just great!

"I'll let you know if Maddie's coming back with me. Maybe you and Sophie can arrange a little get-together so she can meet my friends."

Chapter 31

"Why is Boots growling?" Sarah called to Charles from the living room. He was in the kitchen making a second pot of coffee and feeding Barney.

"I don't know," he responded before turning around. When he did, he realized little Tucker had managed to get onto the counter by the refrigerator and was stretched full length, trying to find a way to climb up the refrigerator. Boots, who had been eating on the top of the refrigerator, had retreated to the top of the cabinets and was looking down at the kitten, her eyes flashing with anger.

"Oh, she's growling because the kitten is trying to get her food," Charles explained.

"What? I've been feeding Boots on the refrigerator so they wouldn't fight over the food. Did you take the bowl down?"

"No, the food is still on top of the refrigerator. Tucker seems to think he can get up there."

By this time, Sarah had come into the kitchen and gasped. "Tucker!" she exclaimed. "Animals are not allowed on the kitchen counter! That's where I prepare our food." She lifted him off and placed him firmly on the floor.

"Meow," he objected.

"Boots gets on the counter," Charles pointed out, supporting Tucker's objection.

"Her feet only touch it for a second on her way up to the top of the cabinets."

Charles reached for the kitten and cuddled him in his arms. "Poor little Tux," he whispered affectionately. "You'll be able to get yourself up there one of these days."

"And Boots will knock him right back down," Sarah predicted. "That is pre-claimed territory up there."

"Poor little thing," Charles repeated in the kitten's ear, which twitched just before he leaped from Charles' arms and landed back on the counter.

Sarah sighed as the kitten again stretched up the side of the refrigerator and mewed pleadingly. Boots turned her back and headed for her corner.

At that moment, the phone rang, and since Charles was closest, he answered it, despite the fact that he knew it was for Sarah. He could see Sophie's name on the display.

"Is she ready to go?" Sophie asked.

"Yes," Charles responded. "Excellent timing. Sarah and I were about to get into it over the house rules as they apply to the animal kingdom."

"Hi, Sophie," Sarah said as she took the phone. "Would you come in the house when you come to pick me up? We have something to show you."

"From your husband's comment, I'm guessing it has to do with an animal. Is Barney okay?"

"Barney is better than he's ever been. Just come on in. The door's open."

Sarah hurried to her sewing room to pick up her supplies and her walker bag instructions. When Sophie arrived, Sarah was holding little Tucker in her arms.

"Oh!" Sophie exclaimed, placing her hand on her heart as she often did when she was touched. "What an adorable little kitten. Where did you get him? Or her?"

"He's a boy. Tucker is his name because he sleeps tucked under Barney's protective arm."

"No kidding? Barney lets him in his bed?"

"He sure does. Tucker is actually another one of Barney's discoveries."

"I remember when he found Bootsy. Where did he get this one?" Sophie asked.

"Barney led us to him in the backyard when we got home from Jason's on Christmas Day. We found his owners and they didn't want him, so he's ours."

"Didn't want him?" Sophie exclaimed, sounding both angry and surprised.

"Actually, he wasn't their cat. He belonged to their elderly mother who had a stroke and can't take care of him. Her son is taking his mother back to Kentucky, but his wife is allergic to cats, so they can't take Tucker."

"Well, that's not a bad reason, I guess, especially since the cat has a good home now. Did they just toss him out?"

"No, he snuck out when the paramedics were there. He was out in the cold for two nights and was delighted to get inside. He's only five or six months old, and he probably had no idea how to survive. He was just lucky that Barney knew he was there and let us know."

Barney watched protectively from the sidelines as the three friends passed the kitten around. The moment Sophie put him on the floor, Barney ran over and poked him toward their bed, where they curled up for an early evening nap.

"We're late for quilt club," Sophie suddenly announced. "Grab your coat and your fabric. I don't want to miss the instructions."

* * * * *

"It looks like everyone is here," Ruth announced. "Sarah, do you want to lead the group with this project?"

"Sure, but I've only read the instructions, and I haven't tried making it, so we'll be figuring it out together."

The group members pulled out their instructions and were reading them over when Frank announced, "If anyone wants to see a finished one, I brought mine." He reached into his bag and pulled out a walker bag that looked like an antique from the Victorian era. His grandmother loved things from the turn of the century, and Ruth had been able to find a piece of reproduction fabric with large peach-colored roses on a dark brown background. She and Frank got together one evening after the shop closed and together they made the bag. They had used a solid brown for the lining since it would show behind the pockets when the bag was on the walker.

"I love the way that dark brown sets off the peach roses," Delores remarked. "Was it hard to make?"

"No," Frank answered. "Ruth did most of it, but I'm going to make another one tonight. Grandma has a good friend named Margaret. She's even older than my grandma, and that's pretty old!" Everyone chuckled. No one had met Frank's grandmother, but they had heard many stories about what Frank called her "old-timey ways."

"So, you want to make one for Margaret?"

"I'm going to try," he responded proudly as he pulled out a piece of multicolored floral and a green that closely matched the leaves in the fabric.

"I love your fabric," Sarah commented.

"Ruth helped me pick it out," he said, smiling in Ruth's direction.

The group began measuring, cutting, sewing, pressing, turning, and topstitching, and in no time, everyone had a long finished piece that looked very much like a table runner.

"Now all we do is fold these ends back and stitch them to form the pockets. Look at your patterns, and you'll see how to do this step."

"What's the Velcro for?" Allison asked.

"It goes on the back and keeps the bag from slipping off the walker," Sarah said as she brought the sample bag over and showed her how it held the bag in place.

"My friend, Paula, made a walker bag for her grandmother," Becky said. "She put ties on the sides to hold it on, and it looked really pretty."

"Clever idea," Sarah responded.

"I think I want to put ties on mine," Frank announced. "Would you show me how?"

Ruth went around the corner into the main shop and got a roll of ribbon that matched Frank's fabric, and Becky helped him attached it to the bag.

By the end of the meeting, everyone had a completed walker bag, and they discussed whether to make more as a charity project. "How many people plan to keep the one they made tonight?"

Almost everyone raised their hand.

"I need one myself," Mabel said. "I still use my walker when I go shopping."

"I want to give mine to our neighbor," Kimberly said. "Don't you think?" she added, turning to her sister, Christina, who nodded her agreement.

"But I could contribute mine," Christina offered.

"I don't really need one," Sarah said, "but it's so cute. I'd like to keep it 'just in case.'" She chuckled.

"Me, too," Sophie said, "but I wouldn't mind making more. Why don't we have one more night like this, and we'd have at least a dozen to donate somewhere."

Everyone agreed, and several people said they were going to make one or two at home as well. Over cake and coffee, they discussed where to donate the walker bags but decided to wait until they were all made before making a final decision.

"Now that was a great meeting," Sophie said as the two friends walked to Sophie's car, hanging onto each other in an attempt to avoid slipping on the ice that had formed while they were in their meeting.

"I'm worried about you getting into your house after you take me home. Should we call Charles and have him meet us at your house?"

"No problem," Sophie declared confidently. She pushed a button on her dashboard, and Norman immediately answered. "I'll be home in ten minutes," she announced.

"I'll be at the curb," he responded.

The look on her friend's face was priceless. *She's in love*, Sarah thought affectionately.

Chapter 32

Weeks passed with no success in locating even one quilt. There were several calls from people who had read the various articles, but most were simply expressing their regrets. They were mostly quilters who understood the impact of losing family quilts.

The *Quilters' News Quarterly* received numerous contacts like the one from Josie Braxton in Texas. The individuals had seen similar quilts, but they all turned out to be false leads but made in good faith.

"There are so many quilts out there that look similar to the untrained eye," Ruth said at their next meeting. "It's no wonder they get so many false leads. I just find it strange that not one single quilt has been located."

"Well, we did find the seven in Hamilton, thanks to Sarah and Sophie," Allison said. "At least I assume we'll get them back eventually, once they finish the Hamilton investigation."

"Isn't it strange that those seven showed up so close to home?" Kimberly commented. "It really makes you wonder where the others are. Are they nearby as well and just haven't been discovered?"

"I think the fact that the seven were found means it's likely that the rest will turn up. At least I like to think that," Delores added.

When asked, Detective Halifax admitted that no real effort was being expended by Middleton PD to locate the quilts and that there wasn't enough evidence to arrest Lonnie Dunkin. "So where do we stand?" Charles had asked.

"If anything comes up, we'll follow through, but we aren't initiating anything at this time. You know, we've had that string of assaults on homeless men over on the south side, and that's taking priority. Why these men choose to sleep on the street in this weather instead of using the shelters is beyond me."

"Sarah says it's because many of these homeless people are schizophrenic and paranoid. They are afraid of the crowded conditions and fearful that something bad will happen to them. Then others have had their meager belongings stolen in shelters, particularly their shoes. I guess some fear the shelters more than they fear freezing on the street."

"Or getting beaten to death by this sick monster that's out there right now," the detective responded.

* * * * *

"Are you up for a little weekend trip?" Charles asked, looking sheepish.

"What do you have in mind?" Sarah asked, remembering that he had promised a getaway after the holidays.

"Well, I was looking at this advertisement for hotel specials in downtown Chicago, and I thought we could drive up on Friday and spend a couple of nights. We could get some of that famous Chicago food and do some sightseeing."

"I didn't realize Chicago was famous for its food," she responded.

"You didn't know that Chicago is sometimes referred to as the 'gourmet dining epicenter'?"

"The epicenter, huh?" Sarah responded. "No, I didn't know that. And what foods make them so famous?"

Charles looked away as he often did when he was teasing her. "Well, there's deep-dish pizza and Chicago-style hot dogs, not to mention their incredible donuts."

"And we're going to drive three hours for hot dogs and pizza?"

"Well, first of all, I don't think you're picturing Chicago-style hot dogs. They are smothered in mustard, onions, tomatoes, and peppers, and they're topped with a dill pickle spear."

Sarah didn't look particularly impressed.

"But that's not really why I want to go. First of all, I found a special on a two-night stay in the Towers. We can get a luxury room overlooking the lake, and their restaurant is known for its *jibaritos*."

"And just what is a *jibarito*?" Sarah asked, raising an eyebrow.

"It's a sandwich served primarily in Chicago's Puerto Rican community, but their chef brought it to the Towers."

"So, we're going for a sandwich?"

"It's not like any sandwich you can imagine. First of all, there's no bread. It's made with tender chunks of steak, melted cheese, lettuce, and tomatoes. And best of all, it's smothered in a garlic mayonnaise sauce."

"And what holds all these ingredients together if they don't use bread?" Sarah questioned.

"Crispy fried and flattened plantains!"

"Hmm."

"Look at the brochure. Here's a picture of the whole meal served with a cheesy beans-and-rice dish and, for dessert, *flan de queso*."

"Which is?"

"A creamy cross between cheesecake and baked custard."

"Charles, there's nothing on this menu that your doctor would approve for you."

"But what about the fact that he said I should treat myself to an occasional splurge? It's good for the soul, he said."

"Your doctor said it's good for the soul?"

"Well, somebody said it. Maybe the preacher."

Sarah laughed. "Well, you got me there. But it still seems strange to drive that far for a sandwich."

"It's not just for a sandwich, hon. I got us tickets to the Broadway Playhouse on Saturday night. It will be a very special weekend."

Sarah laughed and hugged Charles. "You did it again," she said. "I don't know how you come up with these ideas that always sound crazy but turn out to be a fun adventure. When do we go?"

"Tomorrow."

"Tomorrow?" she exclaimed. "Charles, I can't be ready by tomorrow. What about this houseful of animals?"

"Andy is on standby."

"And I'll need to pack."

"Your suitcase is open and on your bed. You only need one dressy outfit and several casual ones."

"And all our medications," she objected.

"Already in our by-the-day containers and ready to drop into the suitcase."

"You've thought of everything."

"I hope so," he responded. "Are you with me?"

She hesitated a moment and then smiled. "Of course I'm with you! I'm always with you."

Chapter 33

"Slow down, Charles. What does that sign up there say?"

"I can't read it yet. It's too far away."

"Pull over, please, Charles. It's advertising an antique show just before we reach Chicago. Why don't we stop and poke around? I really enjoyed doing that in Phoenix, but I was so focused on finding the quilts that I didn't relax and enjoy the experience. We don't have any deadline today, do we?"

"Nope. I've confirmed our reservation, and you said you wanted to have our *jibarito* meal at noon tomorrow instead of tonight."

"Yes, it sounds like a heavy meal, and it would probably keep us awake tonight."

"I agree. So, do you want to stop at the antique show?"

"Absolutely!" Sarah responded eagerly. She reached for the GPS and entered the address on the billboard. "It's about eleven miles from here to the fairground."

"And it's almost lunchtime, so we can have fairground food again. I'll bet they sell Chicago-style hot dogs this close to Chicago," Charles speculated.

Once they were parked and had mapped out their plan for getting the most out of the show, they headed for the first bay. By two in the afternoon, they had visited most of the vendors. They saw an assortment of furniture and household items from the early twentieth century and a few pieces from the 1800s. Charles spent most of his time talking with the vendors and asking questions about how to tell the difference between genuine antiques and the excellent reproductions that flooded the market. He picked up several brochures on markings to watch for.

"Are you ready for some lunch?" Charles asked. "My feet hurt."

"I am, but would you go ahead and order something for both of us? I want to take a look inside that tent. I saw a woman come out carrying a bolt of fabric. I'll meet you at the food vendor in a few minutes."

"Spoken like a woman on a mission. I'll see you sometime later, but I know what will happen if you find a fabric vendor in there."

"Seriously, Charles. I'm just going to take a quick look."

Charles headed for the food vendor, and Sarah entered the tent. It took a few moments for her eyes to adjust to the light inside since she had been in bright sunshine for the past three hours.

Suddenly she thought she saw someone she knew.

"Jeff? Jeff Holbrooke! What in the world are you doing here?" Sarah said excitedly, not expecting to see anyone she knew.

She looked around and didn't see anyone else working at the booth. She only knew Jeff as the administrator of the nursing home and the Community Center. She had no idea he was into quilts and quilting. She hadn't even seen him at their show.

"I didn't know you had an interest in quilts, Jeff. Are you selling ...?" but she abruptly stopped talking.

Quilts were spread out on the table and hanging from the dividers that surrounded the long booth. Beautiful quilts. Old quilts.

"Our quilts!" she exclaimed.

She looked around for Jeff, who had slipped out of sight momentarily, but she immediately felt his breath on the back of her neck. And she felt the cold hard barrel of a handgun pressed against her back.

"Not another word," he said. "Just start walking."

He guided her around the side of the booth and out of the tent through a slit in the canvas. They were facing the back parking lot.

"So you and that nosy husband of yours finally figured it out," he said as he used his gun to push her across the parking lot toward his RV, which was parked near the tree line.

"We didn't figure out anything, Jeff. We're on our way to Chicago and just stopped at the antique show. I just came into the tent to take a look. I didn't expect to see you, of all people, this far from home. What are you doing here?" she added, trying to sound like she didn't know what he was up to.

"Shut up, Sarah. I know better. Your husband has been nosing around the Center for weeks. He's been pretending to investigate Lonnie Dunkin, but I've been onto him for a long time. I saw him looking at the quilt hanging in my office, and I could see the wheels turning. He knew it was me, and he thought he was smart enough to take me down. But he was wrong. He didn't count on me having a bargaining chip."

"What bargaining chip?" Sarah asked, confused.

"You, of course."

He opened the door to the RV and roughly pushed Sarah in, causing her to fall. She struggled to get up, but he pushed her back down with his foot and locked the door. "Stay there. I have business to take care of, and then I'll decide just how to cash in my chip." Then he laughed at his shrewdness.

Sarah tried to get up once he closed the curtain to the back room, but she decided not to anger him. She heard him on the phone but couldn't make out his words. *Perhaps there's some room for reasoning with the man.*

She slipped her hand into her jacket pocket, but her cell phone wasn't there. *Could it have fallen out?* she wondered as she felt around where she was lying. *Charles! Will he come looking for me in the tent? Will he recognize the quilts? Will he figure out where I am?*

She remained quiet and tried to hear what the man was saying. *Something about money. He owes someone money, but why does he sound so desperate? He has a good job. Surely he can pay his bills.*

Holbrook came storming out of the back room, looking angry. "The idiot. He won't listen to reason." He wiped his forehead with his shirtsleeve, and Sarah realized he was dripping with sweat. *This man is more frightened than I am,* she thought and wondered why. The cool, composed nursing home administrator was gone and had been replaced by a man panicked and unsure.

Oh, Charles. Please look at the quilts. I know you'll recognize them. Can you read my mind from that far away? Charles often seemed to know what she was thinking. He sometimes answered her questions before she asked them. *Please look at the quilts. Please recognize the quilts. Please find me*, she pleaded.

Jeff Holbrooke saw that Sarah was now in a sitting position but still on the floor. He decided to let that go. Neither spoke.

He tried to look strong and confident, but he had no idea what to do next. He hadn't expected to get caught with the quilts.

Jeffery Holbrook hadn't planned to take the quilts, but the opportunity was right there, and he knew the cash would buy him some time. He owed the wrong people a great deal of money. He had yanked the quilts off their frames on a whim, and he couldn't believe how easy it was. Within a few minutes, he had them all in his car, and he was driving away. He sold a few to a guy he knew who dealt in stolen merchandise, but decided that was too dangerous. He kept the rest in a storage locker for a couple of months, but as his desperation grew, he knew he had to get his hands on the cash. He found this venue just outside Chicago that was known to be an antique vendors' paradise. He figured he could unload the batch in one afternoon and walk away with an easy ten grand, maybe more.

What were the chances this bitch and her husband would show up? he thought. *Now what?*

"I have an idea," Sarah said in a soft and unthreatening tone. "Would you be willing to hear it?"

"Shut up," the man responded.

"I will, but please just listen for a minute. You and I both have a problem, and I think we can help each other."

Holbrook didn't answer, but he flipped his hand upward as if you say, "Go on," and she did.

"No one but me knows you are here. My husband is at the food vendor, and he thinks I'm looking at fabric. If you let me go, I can simply sit down with him and eat lunch, and you can proceed with your sale. No one need be the wiser."

"How stupid do you think I am, Sarah?"

"I don't think you're stupid, but if we do it this way, you will be safe, and so will I. If I cross you, you know where I live."

"If you cross me, I'll be in prison, and it won't matter that I know where you live."

"If I were stupid enough to have you arrested, they wouldn't keep you long. This is a pretty minor crime in the scheme of things. And I'd be forever in your sights. My life wouldn't be worth living."

"Oh, not your life, my dear. I'd never hurt a pretty lady like you, but that husband of yours—now that's a different story."

Sarah froze. *I've made a deal with the devil,* she told herself.

Holbrook looked at the alternatives. His own life was already not worth living. He owed more money than he'd ever see. This piddly ten thousand wouldn't make a dent in his gambling debt. He had to get out of town. Disappear.

After a while, Holbrook took a deep breath and said, "Okay, Sarah. I'm going to take a chance on you. But we walk back together, and we go straight to the food court and sit down with your husband, and we chat like old friends. You say one word, and I shoot him. You got that?"

"I understand."

"Then you come up with an excuse for why you want to leave, and the two of you drive right out of my life forever. Got it?"

"I understand. Are you going back to your job?"

"Why do you ask that?" he demanded.

"I just thought that it would be uncomfortable."

"You're damn right it would be uncomfortable, at least for you, because this deal of yours isn't just for today. It's forever. One word, and that's all it'll take for you to become a widow."

Sarah gasped, but said, "I understand."

"But I'll answer your question. No, I'm not going back. We'll both be walking away. The only difference is that I'll have the advantage of knowing where you are, so never forget the deal we made today."

"I won't," Sarah responded, trying not to let her fear show.

They walked together toward the food court. The gun was in his pocket, but so was his hand. *Would he fire in this crowd?* she wondered but didn't want to take the chance.

"Jeff!" Charles exclaimed, looking up from his lunch. "What are you doing here?"

"Just on my way to the Windy City," Holbrook responded nonchalantly.

"I was beginning to worry about you, sweetie," Charles said, turning to Sarah. "You look pale. Are you feeling okay?"

"Just a little tired, I think," she replied. "Maybe we should head on to the hotel."

"We sure can," Charles replied as he stood and shook Holbrook's hand. "Good to see you, man."

"It's a small world," Holbrook responded as he winked at Sarah.

Chapter 34

"You've been very quiet," Charles said with concern. "Aren't you feeling any better?"

"I'm fine," she responded. "Let's see if we can walk off that big lunch." Charles agreed that he could certainly use the walk, but he wondered why Sarah thought she'd had a big lunch. She had hardly touched anything on her plate.

Did I do the wrong thing? Should I tell Charles? Sarah was torturing herself with indecision, but she knew if she told him he would call the police and have Holbrook arrested. "... and you will be a widow," Holbrook had said.

The play took her mind off Holbrook intermittently that evening, but fear and indecision washed over her like waves during the night. The next morning she looked pale and haggard. "I'm taking you to the doctor as soon as we get home," Charles announced.

"I'm fine," she said weakly, without looking him in the eye.

After a nearly wordless breakfast, they packed their bags and checked out of the hotel. Charles looked out the hotel windows at the lake, which was as smooth as glass that morning. He started to point it out to Sarah, but she was staring straight ahead, lost in her thoughts and apparently unaware of her surroundings.

After driving a while in silence, Charles turned the radio on and was searching for a music station, but the reception was very poor. Only one station came in clearly, the local news station, so he left it on.

> "The man murdered at the antique show yesterday has been identified as Jeffery Holbrook from Middletown. Police chief Hanson reported today that the crime appeared to be a targeted, professional killing.
>
> "Holbrook was the administrator of the Cunningham Nursing Home and Community Center in Middletown and was on the board of the Cunningham Village retirement community. Mr. Holbrook will be missed by the many residents and patients he has served. Our community is appalled that this could happen to a visitor to our town."

Charles had pulled over to the curb to listen and exclaimed with disbelief, "But we just saw him!" He turned to Sarah and realized all color had drained from her face. She looked as if she were about to faint. "Hon, are you okay?" He reached for her hand, and she leaned into his arms and began to sob.

"What is it? I didn't know you were that close to …" but he realized her entire body was now trembling. He wasn't sure what was going on with her or what he should do. She continued to sob.

"Please take me home," she managed to say, but he thought better of it and drove to the small clinic he had seen a mile or so back. He helped her out of the car; she was still trembling and weak. She leaned against him for support as he helped her walk into the building. He held her in his arms as he asked to see a doctor right away. Her sobs came intermittently.

Charles told the doctor what little he knew, and the doctor, after a brief examination, said she was in shock. He gave her a shot and had her lie back on an examining table until the drug took effect.

"Can you tell me what's going on?" Charles asked gently once she seemed able to focus, and the whole story came pouring out—the fear, the guilt, and the relief.

"It's over, baby," he said, holding her close. "You've been holding all that in? Why didn't you tell me?"

"He said he would kill you if I told," she whispered.

Chapter 35

"We picked up the quilts," Detective Halifax announced when Charles answered the phone. "The other vendors got together and packed them all up and had them ready for us when we arrived."

"And do you agree it was a professional killing?"

"Absolutely. All the signs were there, and an investigation of Holbrook's finances showed him deeply in debt. His ex-wife told us he'd been a compulsive gambler for years. It's what killed their marriage. He probably owed the wrong people."

"Where are the quilts now?"

"I have them, and Hamilton PD brought me the seven they were holding. I'd love to turn them all over to you if that's possible. Ruth said she'd take care of getting them back to their owners, but she was not comfortable after what they've been through. I figured with your background as a cop, you'd be the best person to take charge of them."

"Why do you suppose he sold the seven to the Hamilton shop?" Charles asked.

"Maybe he needed the money right away, and that was all she'd buy. He might have sold them all to her if she'd been willing to buy them."

"You're probably right. He was certainly desperate," Charles responded. "Do you want me to pick them up today?"

"Definitely. Ruth wants to return them during the quilt club meeting this week."

"That's tomorrow. I hope Sarah will be ready."

"How is she?" the detective asked.

"She's been asleep for the past twelve hours, Hal. I think the medication the doctor gave her was meant to help her sleep it off. I spent a whole day with her in Chicago and didn't know what she was holding in. I thought she was coming down with something, but she was in a state of terror—and not for her own life. For mine! That's what makes it so bad. She was suffering because she thought she'd put my life in danger."

"She'll be back to her old self," Hal responded. "She's a strong lady."

"She will," Charles agreed confidently. "Thanks for taking care of getting the quilts to us, Hal."

The phone rang again just as he was hanging up. "Sophie, hi."

"How's she doing?"

"Still sleeping, Sophie."

"Is she going to be okay?" Sophie asked with a quiver in her voice.

"Sophie, she's going to be just fine. It will just take time."

"Is there anything I can do?" Sophie asked.

"Not right now, but I'll call you when she's up and ready for company. I know she'll want to see you."

"Company?" a soft voice behind him asked. "Are we having company?"

Charles was startled and turned to see his wife standing in front of the window with the sun shining across her face. Her eyes were sparkling, and she was smiling. She was wearing jeans and her favorite sweatshirt. She was holding a small furry black and white bundle in her arms.

"I woke up to this little guy licking my face," she said tenderly. Looking into her husband's eyes, she added, "Thank you for taking such good care of me."

"Come sit with me in the kitchen," he said after kissing her cheek and patting little Tucker's tummy. "I need your help. I wanted to make frozen waffles, but I can't find your recipe."

Her laughter was music to his ears.

Chapter 36

Charles called Ruth and confirmed that he would be bringing the quilts to the club meeting that night. She then called everyone to encourage them to come to a party. "I told them we're celebrating the fact that the quilts have been recovered, but I didn't tell them I would actually have them here. Some of the quilters probably figured it out," she said with a laugh. "I just hope everyone comes, so we don't end up with any unclaimed quilts."

"I'll deliver them within the next few days if there's anyone who can't make it," Charles offered.

That evening, he loaded the quilts into his van and, according to Sarah's instructions, placed Andy's quilt on the front seat. He locked the van and then locked the garage door just to be safe before returning to the house.

"Are you about ready?" he called to Sarah.

"Yes, I just have a quick phone call to make."

She reached for the kitchen phone, and moments later Andy answered. He knew the quilts had been recovered but didn't know that they had finally been released by the police. Sarah had gone to great lengths to keep him from knowing. She wanted to surprise him herself.

"I'd like to stop by for a minute before I leave for the quilt club if that's okay with you," she said.

"Sure! Come on by," Andy responded. "Bring the old man if you want."

"I'll do that, but now he's frowning. I have you on speaker, and he heard that disparaging remark."

"I'm not an old man," Charles grumbled. "You'll know when I'm old."

Andy laughed, "Only kidding. So, Sarah, when are you coming by?"

"Right now," she responded.

A few minutes later, Andy opened the door and saw Sarah standing there with his aunt's quilt neatly folded and lying across her arms. "I told you I'd take good care of it," she kidded, referring to the time she had lost his mother's tie quilt, only to find it several months later under the guest bed where Barney had stashed it.

Andy was speechless, and tears welled up in his eyes. "You have her quilt," he muttered barely above a whisper. He gently reached for the quilt and hugged it to his heart. "You know, when Charles called and told me about how it was recovered, I told Caitlyn, but we didn't tell Aunt Maddie that it had been found. In fact," he said with a laugh, "we couldn't tell her since we never told her it had been lost."

"That's probably best," Sarah responded as she followed Andy into his house. She looked around, confused at first, and then remarked, "Your house is the reverse of Sophie's, isn't it? It seems strange to see the hall on that side and the kitchen over there."

"Yes, I always feel a little disoriented when I go into her house," he responded distractedly, still hugging the quilt protectively. "So, were all the others as happy as I am to get their quilts back?"

"They don't have them yet," Sarah replied. "They're all in the van, and we're on our way to the quilt club now to deliver them."

Andy's eyebrows shot up his forehead. "Do you need any help? I'd love to see the quilters' faces when you walk in."

"I'd love the help," Charles said, placing his hands on his lower back and stretching backward as if to get the kinks out. "You don't realize how heavy three dozen quilts can be."

"Come on, old man," Andy responded in jest. "Let me give you a hand."

Before leaving the house, Andy took his quilt into the bedroom, carefully placed it in his footlocker, and attached the padlock. He dropped the key into his jeans pocket. He planned to buy a new bed for his guest room and display the quilt there. He was hoping that Sarah would help him decorate the room around the quilt, but he hadn't discussed it with her yet.

"Where are you going to keep your quilt?" Sarah asked as they were getting into the van.

"Strange that you should ask," Andy responded with a mischievous grin, and while Charles drove, Andy and Sarah eagerly discussed their plans for exploring yard sales and antique shops.

* * * * *

The quilts had been delivered to Charles in three separate packing boxes, each containing approximately a dozen quilts. Charles had brought along his hand truck so that they could carry all the boxes into the shop at once. When they arrived at Running Stitches, Charles parked away from the shop windows so the quilters wouldn't see the boxes being unloaded.

"Ready?" Sarah asked, and Charles indicated that they were. "Let me go in first," she suggested, "and you men follow in a couple of minutes."

"Okay, but come back and hold the door open for us," Charles said.

As Sarah entered the shop, she was shocked to see so many people. It looked like every member of the club was there. In addition, she saw several people she didn't recognize. One elderly woman sitting near the door had a walker next to her chair. Sarah immediately recognized the walker bag and said, "You must be Frank's grandmother."

"I sure am, and you folks have taught my boy so much! I sure thank you all."

"Your grandson is a delight, and we love having him in the club. Where is he now?" she asked.

"He went to get me some punch and a piece of cake. He'll be right back."

Sarah suddenly remembered she was supposed to be holding the door for the men and the hand truck, but she was hoping to get everyone's attention first. When she spotted Ruth, she hurried over and asked if she was ready.

"Tell them to come in," Ruth said, and she simultaneously called out to the group. "Okay, everyone, crowd around the front of the shop. I have news for you. Sophie, is anyone back in the kitchen?"

"No, everyone is out here," Sophie responded, taking a quick look in the makeshift kitchen.

"Okay, Sarah," Ruth said. "Do your thing."

Sarah opened the door, the little bell above the door tinkled, and the men pushed in the hand truck carrying the pile of boxes.

"Quilt delivery," Charles called out for everyone to hear.

There were gasps, whoops, and tears. Suddenly, loud applause broke out as everyone crowded around the hand truck while simultaneously hugging the men who had brought it in. "How can we ever thank you?" one woman asked.

"It wasn't us," Andy said. "We're just the deliverymen. Talk to your gal Sarah over there. She's the one that made this happen."

Charles saw that they were crowding around his wife, inundating her with questions, and he thought he spotted a look of panic cross her face. He hurried to her side and led her off toward the kitchen. "I need a cup of coffee. Honey? Will you show me where it is?" Turning to the group, he said, "Andy here will be unpacking your quilts one at a time. Watch for yours. They're all there!"

By the time Sarah and Charles rejoined the group, Andy was holding the last three quilts. "These are unclaimed," he said to Sarah, looking worried.

"Whose are those?" Sarah asked, turning to Ruth.

"They must be Peggy's," Ruth said. "She had three quilts in the show, but she couldn't make it tonight. They were having a special program at the nursing home, and she wanted to be there with her husband. She said she'd try to stop by later, on her way home."

It made Sarah smile when she noticed that most of the quilters were hugging their quilts to their hearts, just like Andy had done earlier. Frank's grandmother now had four or five quilts on her lap, and Sarah asked if she could open one of them up and look at it. She hadn't had a chance to see them at the show. When she and Sophie held it up, the group crowded around and oohed and aahed. "This was made by my grandmother," Frank's 95-year-old grandmother announced proudly. "Must be near 150 years old by now, don't you suppose?"

"That's about right, Mrs. Franklin," Ruth responded. "I'd say it was made in the mid-1800s."

"Do you quilt, Mrs. Franklin?" someone asked.

"Oh, I did years ago, but mostly I crochet now. I know that's out these days, but I still love doing it. I made collars and cuffs for my grandchildren like I used to wear, but I've never seen them wearing them. I guess that kind of thing is too old-fashioned."

"Let me show you something," Lacey said. She brought her smartphone over and pulled up a site that sold crocheted collars, scarves, and baby clothes.

Mrs. Franklin studied the website carefully. "I don't see any cuffs like I make, but look at these big ones. It says they're boot cuffs," she commented, looking surprised.

"Boot cuffs are very popular, Mrs. Franklin."

"Oh, golly," Mrs. Franklin gasped. "Look at those prices. I should be selling my stuff. Frank, could you help me sell some of my crochet on my computer?"

"You have a computer?" Charles asked.

"Don't act so surprised, young man," she responded defiantly. "Of course I have a computer! I'm not about to let this world pass me by."

Charles looked across the room at his wife and pictured her twenty years in the future. *Yeah*, he thought with a chuckle, *she'll never let the world pass her by either.*

The excitement went on, as did the party. "What's going on here?" Peggy asked as she entered the shop much later. "I was passing by and saw the lights. I thought you'd be closed by now."

"Come get your quilts and join the party, Peggy. We have three dozen reasons to celebrate!"

FRAYED EDGES

See full quilt on back cover.

Andy reconnected with family while exploring the history of his great-grandmother's antique quilt. Make this 84″ × 104″ quilt to add to your family's heritage.

MATERIALS

Light fabric: Scraps to total 1⅞ yards

Dark fabric: Scraps to total 3⅛ yards

Neutral fabric: 3⅛ yards

Inner border: ⅝ yard

Outer border: 1⅝ yards

Backing (108″-wide): 3 yards

Batting: 92″ × 112″

Binding (cut 2¼″ wide): ¾ yard

Project Instructions

Sew fabrics right sides together. • Seam allowances are ¼″.

FOUR-PATCH BLOCKS

Make 128.

1. Cut 256 squares 3″ × 3″ from light fabrics and 256 squares 3″ × 3″ from dark fabrics.
2. Sew together each light fabric square with a dark fabric square. Press toward the dark fabric.
3. Sew together pairs of units, aligning lights next to darks, to complete 128 Four-Patch blocks.

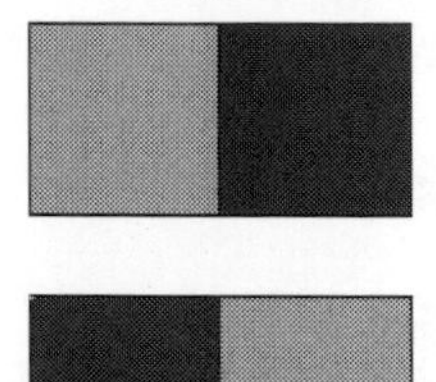

HALF-SNOWBALL BLOCKS

Make 124.

1. Cut 124 squares 5½″ × 5½″ from the neutral fabric.
2. Cut 248 squares 2¾″ × 2¾″ from dark fabrics. Draw a line diagonally from one corner to another on the wrong side of each square.
3. Align a dark square with a corner of a neutral square. Sew on the drawn line. Trim ¼″ from the sewing line. Press toward the dark fabric. Make 124.
4. Repeat Step 3 on the opposite corner of each neutral square to complete 124 Half-Snowball blocks.

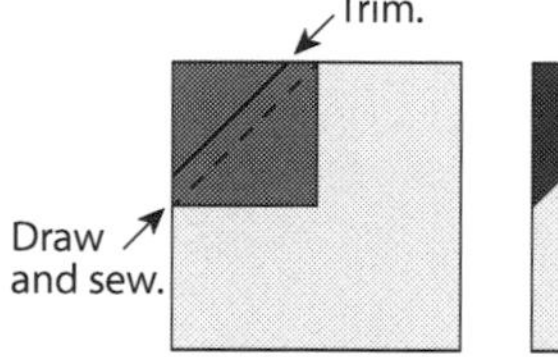

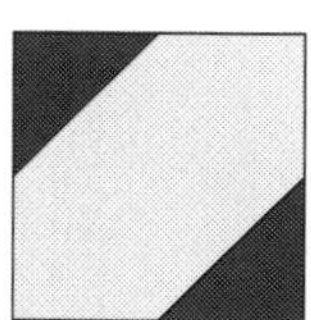

SECTION A

Make 2. Press toward the Four-Patch blocks.

1. Sew a Four-Patch block to the left side of a Half-Snowball block. Orient the Four-Patch with a light square at the *top right* next to a triangle of the Half-Snowball at the *top left*. Make 54.
2. Sew together 3 units from Step 1, attaching Four-Patches to Half-Snowballs to make a row. Make 18.

3. Sew a Four-Patch to the Half-Snowball at the right end of 10 rows.
4. Sew a Half-Snowball to the Four-Patch at the left end of 8 rows.
5. Sew together 9 rows to make Section A. Alternate the rows: The first and all other odd-numbered rows should have a Four-Patch at the left. Make 2.

Section A—make 2.

SECTION B

Make 2. Press toward the Four-Patch blocks.

1. Sew a Four-Patch block to the left side a Half-Snowball block. Orient the Four-Patch with a light square at the *bottom right* next to a triangle of the Half-Snowball at the *bottom left*. Make 54.

2. Repeat Section A, Steps 2–5 (pages 221 and 222), to make 2 Sections B.

Section B—make 2.

ASSEMBLE AND FINISH QUILT

1. Assemble as shown.

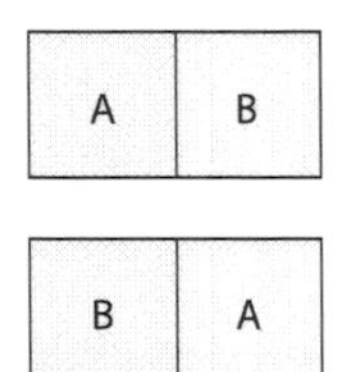

Quilt assembly

2. Add inner borders.

Cut 2 strips 2″×90½″ for sides.

Cut 2 strips 2″×73½″ for top and bottom.

Sew borders to sides and then top and bottom.

3. Add outer borders.

Cut 2 strips 5¾″×93½″ for sides.

Cut 2 strips 5¾″×84″ for top and bottom.

Sew borders to sides and then top and bottom.

4. Layer the pieced top with batting and backing. Quilt and bind as desired.

READER'S GUIDE:
A QUILTING COZY SERIES
by Carol Dean Jones

1. Sophie became very stressed over a potential yet unconfirmed problem in her relationship with Norman. Why do you think she was reluctant to clarify the issue directly with Norman? How does Sophie feel about him? What do you think she really wants from their relationship?
2. Do you have quilts that have been passed down through your family? Do you know the stories of these quilts? Will future recipients of your quilts know their stories? What could be done to preserve the history of the quilts you have made?
3. Aunt Maddie let guilt and regret shape her entire life. How could her life have been different if she had dealt with those issues? How do you think Caitlyn and Andy's presence will change Maddie's life?
4. Charles said that every generation talks about the "good old days" being a simpler time. Do you think it was, in fact, simpler? Will future generations look back and see our times as being simpler?

5. Sarah and Charles went to extraordinary expense to get Barney a pacemaker. A generation ago, most animals were kept outside. What do you think accounts for this change in attitude? Are our pets filling some missing need in our lives? And if so, what?

6. Were you aware of the stolen-quilt network that exists in the quilt community? Have you seen articles in magazines and online with pleas from people whose quilts have been stolen? Have you had a quilt stolen or known anyone who had to search for a missing quilt? What do you think motivates someone to steal a quilt?

A Note from the Author

Writing this series has been a joy. I've met many of my readers through my blog and by email, and you have consistently been loyal, supportive, and encouraging.

What has given me the most pleasure has been hearing from readers who have said that Sarah and Sophie taught them better ways to deal with the many issues of aging. And that was exactly my intention. After thirty years as a geriatric social worker, I had seen seniors giving up and others taking steps to get the most out of their retirement years. I wanted to share what those seniors taught me, and I decided to have Sarah, Sophie, and all their cohorts act it out in this series.

You watched them deal with the many losses of old age, with major health issues, joint replacements, abuse, and Alzheimer's; and you saw them taking positive steps to deal with these problems. But you also saw them having fun, enjoying their many friends, learning new things, and supporting each other. We have all learned from them.

I've also heard from my readers that Sarah and Sophie have become their close friends, and I must admit they have become friends of mine as well.

Thank you for reading this series and for your frequent contacts. Please continue to stay in touch.

Best wishes,

Carol Dean Jones
caroldeanjones.com
quiltingcozy@gmail.com

A Quilting Cozy Series by Carol Dean Jones